I was on my last night of seventeen when I met him. Bryant Crossman was wild, surreally beautiful and devilishly charming. And for one fleeting moment, before I even knew his name, he looked at me like the world stopped and I was all he could grasp onto. Six months later, that's exactly what happened.

Crossed

Samara Reed

Cover by Mae Photographics

2024

Chapter One

"Clary! You came! I thought you might have turned into a pumpkin," Annabelle exclaimed as I walked through the door.

All Cinderella after midnight jokes aside, she was everything a mother wanted in her daughter's best friend, plus a few things she didn't need to know about. Like the parties that started promptly at midnight, never earlier and never a minute later. It was after one AM and the party was already well under way and wouldn't shut down any time soon. Thus, the pumpkin jokes, every time, because I never arrived early during the door rush. Too many people.

"If you didn't run on a vampire's schedule I might attend more of these things at opening time." My reply earned me an eye roll, but I knew that was coming.

"Whatever, you're here now." Annabelle looked me up and down and crinkled her nose. "You. Closet. Now."

"How did I know this was coming too?" I mumbled as Annabelle towed me through the crowd with a few screeches of "Move already!" as she went.

When she clicked the door to her room closed, she slumped against it for a moment, sighing, before plunging into her closet and bursting into conversation, talking a mile a minute as she plowed through hangers. "You really should consider shopping with me. You have those legs for days, girl! All five-seven and slender legs I'd kill for. Why do you insist on covering them in mom jeans when you should be flashing those beauties on the dance floor in a mini! OMG crop top! That's exactly it, show off that adorable belly button ring you got on break for your birthday." She turned around and frowned at me. "Why do you still have clothes on? Strip woman!"

Did I mention this was an intervention? Annabelle liked to 'make-over the nerd in me' as she always so politely put it. We'd done this for almost four years now. I always arrived dressed down cute but comfy, and she would make me up flashy and girly. The skirts really weren't comfy attire.

"Really, Anna, I like my jeans."

"My mom likes your jeans Clarissa, it's a problem. Now take them off and put on this skirt, so when you're shaking your fine little booty on my dance floor, people don't think I dragged you up here and dressed you from my mother's closet. Mkay?" She just stood there and blinked at me with the question still hanging in the air.

I didn't think people really did that. Just blinked at someone. But Anna did, frequently. I burst out laughing while I shook my head at her.

"And then sit here. I'll be right back to rescue your poor hair." She pointed out the chair and rushed out of the room.

I met Annabelle freshman year, when I literally tripped into her and sent the drawing pencils she'd been sorting flying everywhere. I was already late for class, and now we would both be late due to my persistent clumsiness.

"OMG watch where you're walking!" She screeched at me. Then she looked down at my array of books with her pencils among them, sighed, stomped her foot and started clearing the floor. "Why are you in such a hurry anyway? Do you know how late you're going to make me when I would have been perfectly synced with the bell as always since I literally have to just walk across the hall? I should be the one in a hurry, but I hate hurrying. Know why? This is why." She hovered her hands over the mess for effect.

I just stared at her; I couldn't make my mouth work while hers ran on. Annabelle was clearly not cut from the same social circle as me. No. She was way up the chain and I, well, wasn't. I had zero idea how to talk to this girl.

"Helloooooo." She snapped in my face. "It's sweet you apparently think I'm pretty or whatever,

staring at me like that. But this is your fault, remember? Get your books so I can count my pencils and get the F outta dodge."

I hurried to grab everything, muttering my apologies under my breath.

"Yeah, yeah, I get it. Got them all? I've got all of mine. Push up your glasses and watch for people before you make like a meteor again, yeah?" And off she went, ponytail swaying behind her as she disappeared into Mr. Ains' classroom just after the bell. Fifth period advanced drawing. It's the only class he still taught. I knew Annabelle was a freshman because she was in my freshman homeroom. She must be pretty talented to be in advanced drawing as a freshman. I admit I was a little green with envy.

The next morning, she plunked next to me in said homeroom and shoved a notebook into my line of sight. "Clarissa, right? I'm Annabelle, hi."

I adjusted my glasses in a moment of panic. "Um, Clary actually, but yeah."

"Cool. So, I figure you owe me one after running into me like a freight train yesterday. I got

stuck with Brody as a drawing partner because every other easel was full. Do you know how much that boy stares at the goods? Like, you're drawing my face, not my cleavage. Total creep. Anyway, now I'm collecting one favor. Just one. You look smart. Look at those glasses and that cardigan. Adorable, but nerd factor. In a totally cute way. I need you to look at these notes for bio. I cannot bomb this quiz. Last shot sort of thing. Do that and we're square."

Does this girl even breathe? I stared at her for a moment trying to process what was going on while a few kids behind us started whispering and giggling.

"That was an accident. I said I was sorry." I wasn't sure what to make of this. Was it standard protocol to owe a favor for an accident?

"Well, I get that. But this would do me a total solid. Cool?" She looked like a sad puppy.

Who says no to a sad puppy?

"Okay sure. But it really was an accident." As I looked through her notes, I felt a sinking sense of dread. This was all backwards. I glanced at the clock. We had thirty-five minutes to go. "Okay, Annabelle, here's the *thing. You sort of recorded these processes backwards."* See? Dread. Now it was on her face. *"But I think I can explain this to you."* I flipped the notebook around, tore out her notes and started explaining while she took new notes. I had to admit, I didn't think she'd take notes, and detailed ones at that. It struck me as defiant of her almost, to be this studious while understanding she was about to fail when she was the face of popularity.

"Does that make sense?" I asked her as the bell rang, signaling a finality to my lesson. It had to make sense. We were out of time.

"You're like, professional. Seriously. Can you come teach bio? Half the class might not be failing. Ancient relics usually don't know how to connect to teenagers, and it shows." She let out a too loud laugh at her own joke. Heads turning again. She slapped her hand over her perfectly penciled lips. *"This is great. Thank you, you saved me completely."*

She started packing up and I turned to do the same. She turned on her heels suddenly at the door. *"Clary."*

"Yeah?"

"Find me at lunch, okay?"

That's how I met Annabelle Williams. The all the way at the top of the food chain, popular circle floater. She had friends in every group because everyone loved her and her constant cheerfulness. It didn't make me popular or anything. I was still looked at as a nerd. But I really was Annabelle's friend even if they thought I was a charity case and that made me whispered about rather than laughed at to my face. I didn't care. I stood and stared as she walked away that day, totally dumbfounded. The next four years would be a wonderful rollercoaster of friendship that taught me many lessons. Including how to save my hair.

"Voila!" Annabelle said a simple ten minutes later.

I still don't understand how she does it so quickly, but my hair definitely didn't have 'nerd factor' anymore. She French braided the right side then worked the whole thing to float in a tight long braid over my left shoulder and re-curled the ends. It looked sensual and "brings out that gorgeous neck," as she says.

"Cherry Bomb or Vixen?" She questioned, and held up two bright red tubes of lip gloss.

"I don't see the difference."

"Vixen it is then. Trust the artist, this one is much different." She slathered me with lip gloss then pinched my cheeks to bring out a little color; she perfectly curled and lubed my eyelashes and declared herself an absolute genius as she pulled me up off the chair.

"It's the last party of our high school career, Clary, we're all done. So, let's go tear it up, no excuses."

We made our way downstairs, the music vibrated into my feet more prominently with every step I took. The only place I ever really felt like myself all dolled up was in Anna's house. It was dark in there, and loud, and the air was full of alcohol and pot. No one looked at anyone the same way because no one could see you in the same way they saw you under the too bright fluorescents of the too stale classrooms. In there, I was the girl hiding inside of me instead of the one they saw from the outside.

Annabelle beelined for the dance floor when I spotted him and stopped dead in my tracks.

"Anna. Anna! Is that Bryant? Why is Bryant here?" I knew my eyes were bugging out of my head.

Anna just rolled her eyes and followed my line of sight. "Don't tell me you're still hung up on that?" She gestured.

She would never understand. It was at one of these parties six months ago during thanksgiving break, the night before my eighteenth birthday, that Bryant just strolled up to me on a dare, dipped me backwards like we were in a cheesy teen movie and stole my first kiss, in a very passionate way. Not that he knew it was my first kiss. And not that it was a bad kiss. I swear I nearly melted through the floor. It was everything I ever thought a kiss could be. Not that I knew anything about kissing other than what I read in books.

But he didn't go to our school so I had no idea who he was until I tracked Anna down later. And it was a dare. He spent the rest of the night devouring me with his eyes. They smoldered in a way that matched the flame his mouth sparked low in my belly. His irises were so dark I couldn't tell if they were actually pools of black, or if they were stormy blue darkened with the smoky heat he emitted. Every time I felt his eyes on me, they drew me to him. A pull in my core I could feel but couldn't see.

"It's the way he looks at me," I said. That wasn't untrue. Even then, his eyes lingered, and I swear they could see right through this ridiculous, too short skirt. I pulled at it. It didn't help cover me. Anna was almost three inches shorter than me, and it was quite literally made for her.

"Stop futzing. If you still want that, go get that. Because judging by the look on that man's face. That still wants you." Annabelle proclaimed as she sauntered away into the arms of Tawny, her newest fling. She was even shorter than Anna, perky and small chested. Not Anna's usual choice of busty bad asses, but she was so vibrant she was practically a beacon and Anna was completely smitten with her.

I watched them and admired how their smiles melded together adorably as they whispered to each other when I felt an arm snake around my waist as a pair of lips pressed to my neck, feather light but meaningful nonetheless. I gasped and turned, only to run straight into the chest of Bryant Crossman whose lips descended on me once again.

Chapter Two

I stumbled backward a step from the impact of my spin, yanking my lips from his, and he pulled me in tighter.

"Whoa!" his voice drawled out, smooth as the whisky I smelled on his breath. "Easy little gazelle. I have a feeling those aren't actually your shoes." He pointed at the offending footwear with the completely unnecessary heel as a smile lit up his face.

Why Annabelle thought I needed heels for her house parties was beyond me. I never managed to make it through a night in them without either breaking something I stumbled into or stepping on someone, and I was already plenty tall.

"Ah, no. Sorry."

"Don't be, I've got you. I shouldn't have snuck up on you like that. It's just—" He pulled my braid off my neck where it landed in his way. "You have such a gorgeous neck. I couldn't help but sneak a taste." He leaned in again.

"You have an interesting way of asking permission," I snapped as I pushed against his chest. He eased his hands off my back and put them up.

"Sorry. I'm sorry. I'm a little tipsy, and I remembered that kiss we shared, and I got a little bold. Here. Let me start again." He held out his hand. "I'm—"

"I know who you are," I bit out. "You're Bryant. The dick that kissed me on a dare. Also without my permission I might add. A little drunk that night too?"

His smile, quirked up on one side with his raised eyebrow, would be adorable if I wasn't so peeved at the moment. "As a matter of fact I was stone sober that night. That was all me."

His confident tone didn't escape me, it whooshed around in my stomach like the bright blue waves I could see clearly in his eyes tonight even in the dim light glowing from the DJ booth.

"Clary, right? Annabelle's told me a lot about you. How about a soda, Clary? If I remember her run on sentences right, you don't drink much." He held his hand out to me, stayed a step away and gave me distance. I stared at it, skeptically. It wasn't lost on me that this could be another dare.

It also wasn't lost on me that it had been a whole six months since my last kiss, which was my first kiss, and my lips tingled like they knew my next kiss was on its way. Or that Annabelle talked to him about me enough that he knew to ask for a soda.

"Hands off, promise." His outstretched hand waited.

"Yeah, sure." I looked over my shoulder at Anna as Bryant tucked my hand into his elbow and placed his other hand over it. She gave me a thumbs up. How refreshing.

"It looks like your friend likes me," Bryant mused into my ear. He had a huge smile on his face and I spotted a dimple I hadn't seen before now. It was sunk deep in the short stubble in his cheek. I followed it down his jaw and over to his full lips. The bottom one was almost a perfect pout with a small white scar running along one side, the other was bow shaped and both glistened slightly like he licked them recently. The man had deep, sensual eyes and sinfully beautiful lips.

I shook the thought out of my head. I didn't need to go there.

"She likes everyone, why do you think she throws these things? Definitely not for the morning clean up." I was typically nominated to help on that team.

"I thought maybe it was to have an excuse to dress you up. I'm not complaining, but the cardigan from earlier was cute."

I studied him, unable to tell if he was making fun of me or if he had actually been interested from the time I stepped in the door. So, I left it to rest, I didn't want to know. He grinned at me, but it seemed like he was always grinning at something.

"So you didn't just graduate with us yesterday. Where are you from?" I decided to go with the you've-had-your-tongue-in-my-mouth-now-tell-me-abo

ut-you approach. It seemed completely appropriate for

the moment.

His hand wrapped around the back of his neck

as he let out an awkward chuckle. "Ah. Grosson,

actually."

"Grosson as in the private academy uptown? As

in the twenty-five thousand dollars a year to attend,

private academy? That Grosson?"

"That's the one." He was sheepish. I understood

why. We were definitely not a private academy crowd.

You had to be wicked smart and way more well-off than

anyone around here could afford to even think about

getting in there.

"Nice to not have to overwork your brain for a

while talking to us or what?"

He stared at me for a beat as if he could see past

my shield and read my thoughts. "I'd venture to guess

that talking to you for a while would be quite an

exercise. I actually enjoy the people here. The rich kids

in this town aren't always all they're cracked up to be.

Too many toys but still so little fun to be had. Well.

Some of them anyway." He looked offended by his own words for a moment before shaking his head.

"Bryant, I'm... I'm sorry. That was harsh of me. And wrong."

I didn't get a chance to get a further thought in as Savannah bounced into me and spilled her drink all over Annabelle's leather skirt. The cool liquid and the remainder of the ice ran down my legs and into my shoes. It stunk. What was in that thing?

"Whoops," she snickered, then spun in front of Bryant blocking most of my view and turned her cup upside down once more. "I was drinking a powder puff but, oh look, my cup is empty. I'm so parched. Wanna grab me another one?" She twirled her pink tipped hair in her fingers and swayed her shoulders around like she was a prized peacock. A forced, short giggle made its way out of her as she moved forward into Bryant's personal space.

I must've made a face because Bryant burst out laughing and shook his head as I walked away. I only made it a dozen steps before he was behind me again, both my elbows in his hands, and spun me around.

"Seriously, don't let that little display get you down. I'm definitely not that kind of guy. Where are you off to? I didn't get to get you that soda."

"My, aren't we persistent? I need a new skirt." I pulled one arm from his hand and pointed at the other one he still held.

"Sorry, there's something about you that just feels so familiar, it's intriguing. And I'm not used to—"

"Girls not falling at your feet?"

His head tilted to one side while he analyzed me. "Yeah. That too. But I was going to say 'people puzzling me.' I can't read you Clary, and I want to." His thumb stroked my remaining elbow. I looked down at it and wondered again if it was another dare.

"I'm not a book, Crossman," I deadpanned, turned my back to him, and pulled my arm away from his electric touch. I needed to put my mom jeans back on and go home.

Chapter Three

My phone rang. I couldn't answer it. It was across the river on the opposite beach, and I was in the water with nothing but a piece of a giant cardboard box somehow holding up well despite the water all around me.

How would I make it there? Better yet, why did I care at all? It was warm despite the rain. I could walk to shore and lay in the sun, it was only a few feet away and oddly it definitely was not raining there, I wasn't that far in the surf.

Another droplet hit my nose, ice cold and piercing.

Wait. It's raining?

I jumped awake to the sound of my phone ringing. I scrambled over the bed to grab it off the charger. Great, Annabelle.

"Woman, I've called you six times! Why'd you dip out last night? One minute Mr. Dreamboat is escorting you rather politely off the dance floor that you didn't even dance on, and the next, you're just gone. *Poof*! He said something about Savannah being a massive wad and you leaving. What happened?!"

It was only eight in the morning, and she was already in super sonic full story mode. I couldn't count the words that had sped out through the grogginess I felt. Not that I ever really could anyway. I squeezed the bridge of my nose; I could not get a headache so early in the day.

"Savannah intentionally dumped this God awful fruity drink all over me, something about a cream puff. Then she tried to show Bryant her total package, and I just didn't want to deal with it all night. You know how she gets when she sets her sights somewhere. Doesn't she have a boyfriend? Whatever." I sighed. "I dropped your skirt off in the after hours box at the dry cleaner on my way home. It was totally sticky."

"Girl forget the skirt! I want to know what was so rudely interrupted. Dish!"

"We got as far as 'Hey I'm filthy rich' before I got puffed. Those things smell like fairy barf, by the way." Annabelle burst out laughing on the other end of the phone.

"And yet everyone loves them. The powder puff is always the first jug empty. I seriously never told you Bryant is an uptown kid? How'd I miss that?"

"I don't know. How do you even know the guy?" The kids uptown hardly ever make their way to downtown. It's all industrial blocks and mom and pop pizza places until the farmland kicks in, there's nothing for them to do.

There's nothing for us to do either.

"Oh! He paints! Yeah! Remember that class my gran bought for me for Christmas junior year? It was more of a closed session kind of thing, there were only five other artists there. Bryant was the only other person anywhere near my age, and we totally clicked. He's so thoughtful, and hilarious too. And I think he likes you. He kept asking me for over an hour if I'd checked in on you and if you were okay. I figured you'd gone to bed, didn't want to disturb you."

"Well thanks for that. You know me."

"Yeah, yeah, Sleeping Beauty. Anyway, I gave him your number. I told him he could check on you himself. Toodles!"

And before I could get a single sound out after processing what she had said, she hung up.

"Damnit, Annabelle!" I yelled into the blank phone screen before throwing myself against the pillows. Well. Happy Saturday to me.

It was just after one when my phone lit up again on the arm of the couch where I landed for a little Netflix therapy. I expected it to be Annabelle, having finally gotten more than two hours of sleep and wanting to go over what we already talked about that morning.

What I didn't expect was a text from "Mr. Dreamboat" himself.

A shake. It would be Tom's ice cream shop. Interesting pick. Almost old school. But did I want to go there with Bryant? In town it was sort of a couples spot, or a dinner spot for families. I would be leaving in three months to move across the country for college. Was it wise to send any kind of signal to Bryant who, according to Annabelle, liked me? Or worse, get attached. I know what she would say. She would say, "Shut up and get you some, Clary!"

I clicked save number on my phone and typed in something simple: Cross.

A heard a distant 'ping' before a knock on the door sounded. Confusion settled as I passed over to the front door and grasped the handle. I just about died when I swung it open and realized Bryant stood on the other side. After a horrified second, in which I'm sure my eyes were giant brown saucers I could pull a stellar signal from, I shoved the door closed and spun around to lean on it.

I heard his laughter on the other side as he knocked again.

Okay Clary, think.

I pulled my fingers through my hair and tied a small knot in the back of my oversized t-shirt. Why can't I just get dressed on the weekends like, ever? Pulling the door back open I plastered on the biggest smile I could muster. "So, I guess that means you're ready now?"

His low laughter filled my ears again and danced around in my chest. "Yeah, I mean, unless you want to play a round of knock, knock again?"

"What? I, no, I'm—"

"Clary! Relax. It's okay. I got your address from some kid at the pizza place who said you tutor his little sister after he heard me talking to Annabelle about you.

I showed up totally unexpected. It's cool. It was worth it for the look on your face."

I scowled at him. I didn't know if he thought he was being funny, but I also hadn't decided if he was actually funny to begin with. I flashed back to his cockiness the night before. "So, what did you need?"

"I'm here to pick you up for ice cream! Grab your shoes." The grin was back. I was starting to like that grin as infuriating as it also was. I tried to be weary of it, and it was warming me to him.

I peeked down at myself, and his gaze followed. "I have to change. I can drive myself. I'll meet you there." I started closing the door only to find Bryant's hand on mine. I froze. Why did his touch do that to me?

"I could come in and wait a few minutes if that's okay with you?" I looked at him, looking at me hesitantly as though I might disappear if he had given me the chance. He cleared his throat and put his hands up. "I promise I'll stay wherever you put me and keep my hands to myself."

Bryant Crossman, in my house? I barely knew the guy, but Annabelle trusted him. Enough to tell him she was having a party in her house. What am I saying? She lets everyone into her house for parties. But she gave him my number, so that must count for something.

I pulled the door back open all the way so he could come through, "Sure. Come on in."

He ducked his head and walked past me into the hallway. I closed the door and tried to brush past him to lead the way. The back of his hand connected with my bare thigh right where my shorts ended. Sparks of electricity zinged down my leg and into my toes. "Sorry," he ground out, "tight space." But the smile on his face gave him away. He wasn't sorry at all.

"Okay so this is our sitting room. I'm going to pop upstairs and change clothes. I'll be right back. Just, sit, or something."

I turned and fled as I heard a low, "Yes, ma'am" on another laugh. I dialed Anna while I ran up the stairs. She answered with an irritated, 'speak', after five rings. "He's here."

"Hello to you too, Clary. Good morning on this annoyingly bright day. Or is it afternoon? Doesn't matter, you woke me up, it's morning. Who's where?"

"Bryant! He's here. In my sitting room. Waiting for me to change clothes so we can go to Tom's because our conversation was interrupted."

"Whoa! What are you going to wear? Don't wear mom jeans! Please don't wear mom jeans."

I closed the door to my room a little more zealously than I intended and booked it to my closet. No mom jeans. That's easier said than done. I pulled cardigan after cardigan out and threw them on the bed. Formal dresses were too formal for a diner, tank tops needed a cardigan with the coastal weather so finicky in early summer, turtle necks are probably too *turtle-necky*. And there it was: a pale yellow half sleeve sundress with light blue dye in the darting on the waistline. A blue jean jacket was draped over the hanger, they always made such a great pair. That would do perfectly.

One pair of flip flops, a rushed goodbye to Anna and a quick brush of my teeth later and I raced down the stairs. Bryant existed in my house alone longer than I liked to think about.

I found him standing with his back to me, facing the mantle with all my photos hanging above it.

"You're just as adorable now as you were then." He declared to the wall, and pointed at a picture of a seven-year-old me complete with frizzy curls bursting out from my head. When he turned and looked at me there was a moment of surprise on his face before his amusement stepped back in. "Though I do think that your tamed curls are quite a bit better than those. I can't help but think she looks a little more free."

"Ah, yeah. That would be Anna's work. You should've seen the even bigger mess those curls were freshman year. She saved me from myself as she likes to call it. It turns out all a girl really needs is a good conditioner, some serum, and a bowl."

His gaze traveled quickly over my head to where the ends of my hair fell just over my breasts then traveled over the slightly puffy sleeves and landed on my waist. "Well, she did a nice job, I will say. I'd pay to see it wild too. But this! You look fabulous in that dress, and your hair is beautiful too. Now," he put a hand on my waist, and spun me in the opposite

33

direction, and planted a kiss on my shoulder, "let's go get some ice cream."

Chapter Four

I couldn't believe the thing I sat in. I swear the leather on just the seat was more expensive than all of the name brand shoes Anna had spilling out of her closet put together. And that was saying something considering Anna had never put a single paycheck anywhere other than her closet in the four years she worked as a barista.

The underside of the dash glowed a faint lavender color and there was a speaker softly playing indie pop from the cushion just behind my head. Bryant opened his door, plopped in, leaned over the center console, and checked my seatbelt.

"So Clary with the tamed curls, what do you like to listen to?" His hand hovered over the satellite button.

"This is good actually. I like pop. Or classical. I even rebel a little and listen to nineties grunge sometimes."

His eyebrows quirked. "Well, well, well. Isn't that an interesting tid-bit? Indie it is since this station is gold. Here we go!"

We chatted about the party, and how Bryant practically ran to escape Savannah most of the night until he finally called it quits and headed to the pool house where apparently he stays when he comes to Annabelle's parties. Which explained why he was still in my part of town.

"I bet she was pretty irritated by your evading by the end of the night. Savannah usually gets what she wants or everyone hears it. I'm surprised she didn't follow you right into the pool house."

"Yes, well, she's not even remotely interesting to begin with. I've had that conversation already and I don't care to have it repeated." He grinned that grin again, laced with mischief. "And she came with a date, which makes her doubly uninteresting. He got too drunk and passed out on the couch, and she made her way to interrupt us. Not cool. And I locked myself in the pool house. She would have had to beat the door down, and I get the impression she doesn't like to break a nail." He switched off the engine and got out; he jogged around the car to my side. When I tried to grab the handle he *tsked* his finger at me. I was confused for a moment until he swung open my door and held out his hand. "You didn't really think I'd let you open this door did you? What would my reputation look like then? Charming. Dashing looks. Hilarious. Doesn't open the door. What a travesty."

Surprised, I let him pull me to my feet and close the door behind me. He reached forward and adjusted the collar on my jacket; his hand brushed below my ear and sent shivers down my spine. His skin had an effect on me, a dangerous one.

Without a word, his hand found the small of my back and steered me into the ice cream shop. Suddenly, it all felt like a monumentally bad idea. I had no doubt it would be a wonderful, but very, very bad ending that would destroy me.

***

"So ice cream cones and a walk on the boardwalk and then he just brought you home? No kiss at the door even? Just a 'thank you for coming with' and a peck on the cheek?" Anna was doing the blinking thing again, still leaning in to hear every not so juicy detail I was willing to dish to her. Unfortunately for her, there weren't many to serve up.

"Yeah! He was so sweet! He said he'd be back Friday for some art exhibit and asked me to come along. It was nice, really."

"The fundraiser for the shelter? I didn't know he was going to that. Wow. So gentlemanly. Why can't any guys I go out with be like that?"

I raised an eyebrow and looked over my glasses at her.

"Yeah. Don't answer that. Definitely why I play both sides."

"Anyway. I need something fancier than a sundress to wear to the fundraiser. Can I borrow something?" I asked.

Annabelle hopped up and down then scampered to her closet. "Woman, I've got you. I love it when you ask."

We spent the next hour trying things on before settling on a midnight blue calf length dress with shimmer woven into the fibers. The effect of the shimmer on the dark base was mesmerizing, all of the delicate, tiny strands of shimmer thread flashed against the light every time I shifted. It had silver sparkly spaghetti straps and a deep dip in the back. The look was complete with a tiny matching handbag and black slingback heels.

"Bryant's not going to be able to pick his jaw up off your front porch when he sees you in this." She stood behind me, peering at me in the mirror over her shoulder. She tugged gently at my unruly curls and pulled them straight like she was willing them to stay. "What about this? Should I come straighten them on Friday?"

I stared at myself in the mirror.

"Actually, I think I'll just put a touch of mousse in it. Let it get a little wild. This dress calls for some sass, I think. And contacts."

"All jungle woman. I like it." Annabelle launched herself into makeup. She rifled through her drawers, picked out different shades and demonstrated where to put them. I declined all but the lipstick. Bryant said he thought seven year old me looked more free. I was really beginning to like Bryant. Let's see what he thought of me when I was just being me in a fancy dress.

***

I sat in my own mirror on Friday arranging my hair when I heard the knock on the front door. The muffled sound of my parents as they moved through the downstairs hall followed right behind it and the familiar gait of my dad on the tile in front of the door echoed up the stairs. Dad was as burly as a grizzly bear but as sweet as a teddy bear as long as he found you acceptable. It was this reason he insisted on answering the door exclusively.

I stayed true to what I said about my curls. I strategically moussed a few areas, just enough to keep my head from going full Bozo then pulled a diamond studded headband out of a drawer. I carefully placed it between ringlets to hide in my hair and just shimmer.

A quick count to forty, and I heard footsteps coming up the stairs. My father had a longer gait than my mother making it easier to win in the mad dash they made to each be first, but she was usually only about thirty seconds behind him to the door.

A soft knock was the only warning to the knob turning. My mother let out a soft sigh as she entered. "Clarissa! You look so beautiful! And grown up!"

"Thanks, mom. It's one of Annabelle's dresses. I'm going to a fundraiser art show. I thought maybe it called for something a little more fancy than my jeans."

"Oh! Yes! There's a young man downstairs asking for you. Is he taking you to the fundraiser? He's very handsome, as is the car parked in the driveway and the suit he's wearing."

I turned around to look at her. She had a grin on her face but was still looking at me pointedly.

"If you think that's impressive you should see the inside of the car," I muttered.

"You've seen the inside before? Clary, I know we haven't had a lot of discussions woman to woman, especially since we haven't really had a need to discuss boys, and I know you're almost nineteen now, so you are a woman, and I'm certain you have friends who talk about things," she took a deep breath before continuing, "but if you find you need to talk about anything—"

"Mom, I don't. And I know. If I do. But I don't." Was it getting hot or what? I was suddenly very warm in my very tiny dress.

"Okay. Well, then get your tush down there and wow your very attractive date. And make him behave. Because I might be forty, but really I'm still twenty, and I refuse to be a grandma at twenty." She walked away loudly laughing at herself. I scooped up the tiny purse that was supposed to hold all my belongings, but could barely even hold my cell phone, and followed her down the stairs.

When I hit mid-landing, I caught my dad's eyes right as they bugged out of his head. "Whoa." Bryant exclaimed as he stepped out from behind him.

I stopped a foot short of him, and he tipped my chin up from where I was looking down at his feet.

"That's better," he said a moment before he brushed his lips over my cheek. "You look exquisite. Own it like the queen you are."

I smiled up at him.

Handsome Bryant Crossman with his tidal wave eyes and that sexy white scar on his lip stood in front of me and called me a queen. My chin tingled where his fingers still touched it.

"You're too beautiful to look down at the floor."

My father cleared his throat, loudly. "Clary, you look wonderful. I was just telling Bryant here that we have a curfew in this house. It's now eight PM, I understand this gallery thing starts at nine and is for charity. So you can be home at twelve instead of eleven. And I must say Bryant, how refreshing it is to hear a date is for charity. Doing well for the world does well for us all."

My mom smiled at my dad and squeezed his arm softly.

"Okay get out of here before I change my mind about that dress. Drive my daughter safely, I wrote down your plates, and she is to come back the same way she left," my dad commanded..

Bryant looked to me then back to my dad. "Yes, sir."

My dad nodded and stifled a grin. I imagine Bryant didn't deal with a lot of dads like mine.

We rode in silence the first few blocks uptown then Bryant dipped his head in my direction. "So, your dad. He's ah—he's kind of intense, yeah?"

My turn to try to hide a grin. "You could say that."

"He wanted my address. And wanted to know where my dad works. And how long I've been driving and what sort of insurance I have. And if I have any kids."

"NO! He did not ask you that last one."

"Uh-huh, he did. I think he ran out of things to ask me. Then he started asking about where we were going. He seemed sort of excited at the idea of this being a fundraiser."

"I imagine he would be. My dad grew up poor. Like, poor poor. When my grandma lost their house after my grandpa died his aunt took them in. He was thirteen. She ran a women's shelter, and they really needed help. So, his aunt said they could stay with her as long as they both agreed to work for her. She would pay my grandma for them both, and my dad's money was to be saved, so he could start ahead when he was old enough. He never forgot that. How he was fortunate enough to survive and thrive where so many others never did because one person thought it was important to help."

"That's intense, and wonderful of his aunt. I bet he really cares about her." He reached his hand from the shifter to my hand in my lap.

"Yeah. She and my grandma still live and run the shelter together. I volunteer sometimes during the week. They do really great things to help people. Especially the children."

He looked at me and grinned before returning his eyes to the road. "Maybe I can come help sometime. I love to get involved."

"Yeah? That would be great!"

"Then it's settled. You and I have another date." He beamed his million-watt smile out the front window as he flipped his blinker on, and we pulled into the driveway of the gallery, still hand in hand.

Chapter Five

My head spun as we entered the fundraiser. I couldn't quit looking at the beautifully painted ceilings in this building, or the perfectly polished ornate floors, or the leaded glass windows dripping in ivy vines—inside! I'd never been somewhere so exquisite in my life, or where plants grew on the walls on the inside like it was just any old thing.

Bryant kept his hand at the small of my back as we made our way through check in, grabbed our donation vouchers for each of the art pieces, and ordered sodas from the bar.

He led me across the room to the front of the gallery while he explained how the voucher system worked. Each visitor had a ticket with their information on it for each of the displayed pieces. To place a bid, participants would scan their voucher at one of the stations throughout the room and punch in their offer. The box would register the offer and display the current selling price of the piece without giving away the bidder's name. At the end of the evening, each winner will be notified of the pieces they won, and they could come back to get them the next day if they'd already left. The gallery had their payment information on file for easy close of the transaction.

It all sounded absolutely thrilling, and *very* expensive.

We walked the room arm in arm, stopping at each piece to discuss the brush strokes, the mood, the color choices and to give it a story. Some stories were happy and a little ridiculously dreamt up between us, some a little more somber. When we stopped at a rather large, dark piece, I was completely stumped. The piece contradicted itself, and I didn't know what to make of it.

The shapes looked like people, but more like their auras lit up yellow and green and pink against the dark burgundy background. They seemed to be embracing but not touching at the same time. They were turned into one another, locked in each other's gaze instead. Unwavering and full of lust. They didn't look sad, but the mood was intense; the colors a confusing contrast.

"What do you think? What's this story?" Bryant's hand skimmed up the seam in the back of my dress to caress a small, bare patch of skin. Shivers crept through my spine and up my neck, my back flexing of its own will to press closer to his hand.

"I think they're lovers, or maybe they will be. Their stance is like a dance, the beat of the song sending them deeper into each other's being. See the auras? They mean something in this moment. It's sad, but alluring, almost erotic. I wonder what happens when the song is over."

"What do you think might happen when a song like this one ends?" He asked, his voice even but still piqued in interest.

"What makes it an ending?" I inquired. "Is it the eruption after a crescendo and a drift apart until the music slows and stops, as they stop and fade with it? Or is it just the light around them growing and melding together? Do they become one in the end?"

Bryant's hand stilled at the V on the dress, his fingers just below the hem on my tailbone. Goosebumps broke out over my back and legs when he slid them along the seam. A low tingle told me what he thought without even needing to look at him because my body thrummed the same way. I hadn't taken my eyes off the painting, but I chanced a peek in his direction. Bryant's gaze burned into me. A furious storm in his eyes trained on my lips.

"Should we test the theory, Clary?" he asked, voice low between us as he turned and his eyes caught mine. "The music is playing, intensifying. We're dancing, spinning, politely walking to the beat our hearts are drumming out."

He walked me backward as he spoke. One hand on the small of my back still below the V riding my hips and bunching in the fabric like he could push his hand right through it, the other caught behind my ear in my hair. "We can spin and spin, neither too far apart to miss the heat we're creating nor too close to feel the burn of the flames between us."

At that moment, we broke through a set of curtains I swore was a wall. It opened into a garden terrace, and a chill coursed through me as the cold night air hit my skin. Bryant pulled my hips into his and lowered his forehead to touch mine. "How about it, Clary? Can you still hear the music? Are we dancing?" His breathing was ragged; his words had the same low fervor.

"Are you saying the painting is us?" My eyes bounced between his and tried to decipher the shift in him.

"The painting is called *False Dare*." He replied before his lips crashed onto mine. Suddenly, Bryant was everywhere. His hand moved to the back of my neck to pull me in and hold me steady while his other hand snaked up around my hip and squeezed before surging down to my thigh to pull it up against him. When he was satisfied I was close enough, both arms closed around me and his hands roamed my open back before settling on my shoulders, firm and commanding.

I pulled back for air, and Bryant drove his head into my neck, sucking and lavishing my skin. When one hand reached down and grabbed my ass, I jumped with a squeak. Bryant laughed and shushed me.

"We really aren't supposed to be out here." He mused, and backed me to a wall inside the shadows. "I couldn't resist you one more moment though. Talking about us like that."

His mouth came back to mine as he pulled my dress up to secure both my legs around his waist and pressed himself in another step.

"I had no idea it was about us." I murmured between breaths. "Why is it called *False Dare?*"

Bryant brought his gaze back to my face. "Because that kiss wasn't a dare. Someone just said that at some point after, and I let everyone believe it. I kissed you that night because I couldn't think of anything else once I spotted you. Your presence consumed me. Every time I tried to focus somewhere else I found myself searching for you. If I didn't kiss you, touch you, your mere presence in that room was going to burn me alive."

One hand held me up while the other roamed up my thigh in circles, sweeping over my skin as though he were painting every inch of it. "When I saw you again at Anna's party the other night, I felt that same fire burning, and I couldn't keep my eyes off you then either. I had to touch you again. Feel your skin and know I wasn't so drunk that I was imagining you. I didn't think I would get so caught up in it that I would keep craving more."

He reached my bare bottom with one hand and caressed it while our tongues entwined together. "You okay? You're historically very vocal about touch. Is this okay?"

"Bryant," was all I got out before the gallery noises inside suddenly wafted outside. Bryant froze and pressed me impossibly tighter to the wall, his finger moving up to his lips to shush me as a huge smile slowly crept across his face. His shoulders quaked as he tried to hold in a laugh.

A flashlight jumped around. Security. Had they spotted us leaving the gallery? Bryant's forehead dropped to mine, and we paused there, silent, caught up in each other's breath and body heat—just like his painting. The noise from the gallery grew louder before quieting; we were alone once more.

Bryant slowly lowered me to the ground, dragging his hands along my body as I went. "We should go back inside." He pulled my face up to clasp his lips on mine again. His tongue brushed my lips, seaking entrance. I opened and he ventured inside before he trailed kisses over my cheek to my jaw. "Yeah. Here, we're going." He took a few steps backward, lips returning to mine, still exploring. He pulled away finally and gasped for air. "You're absolutely addicting. What the hell am I going to do?"

He raked a hand through his hair and rolled his shoulders. A giggle escaped my lips.

"Well, Mr. Crossman. If you keep that up, we both may have an issue." I strode forward and through the curtain. I glanced over my shoulder to see Bryant watching me, a mix of bewilderment and lust on his face before he quickly stuffed his hands in his pockets and followed.

I had just secured my painting in the backseat and climbed in the front. Yes, my painting. The painting of us, in which Bryant insisted he purchase for me even though he created it. "But it's for charity. Come on, I have to buy something. I want you to have this if you like it, you keep coming back to it."

It was rather beautiful, and I knew exactly where to hang it. The whole thing just seemed ludicrous to me. But Bryant's excitement spurred me on, and I agreed to make a bid on the painting along with a sizable donation of my own from my weekend photo gig savings so he wasn't solely paying for his own painting. And that seemed to have pleased him, too.

"Tell me something about you," he said as we made our way through the driveway and down toward the street. The line out was long.

"Like what?" I put my hand to my chin and stroked it like I was lost in thought. "I don't like peas. I hate carpet. My favorite scent is the smell that fills the air when someone is drying their clothes."

He raised an eyebrow at me. "That's an awfully specific scent."

I shrugged. "It reminds me of my grandma. On the weekends, I would sometimes go with her to clean the laundry mat. That's a smell that stays with you, and you smell it often enough walking through any neighborhood to get nostalgic."

"Fair enough. But no, tell me something real."

"Those were real. I, *hm*. This isn't my dress."

His laughter filled the car. "Well no kidding, I knew that. It's too much for you. But you do look amazing in it. From the looks of that incredible back slit and all that sparkle, it's probably Annabelle's. Great choice though, it looks like it was made for you. And I love that your eyes are free from your glasses tonight, they're so clear and bright. No, tell me something true. Something deep. Something that's just you, and no one else."

I paused. Something that's only me. What was only me? I spent four years being Annabelle's best friend. That's how so many people talked to me. 'You're Annabelle's friend, right?' That was my current identity. We did everything together, in twin mode. The same movies, the same music (mostly), the same parties, which were usually hers. We're even going to the same college in a few months. Something only me was hard to dig for.

"You were my first kiss."

Bryant's head whipped around, "What? No way. Please tell me that's a joke."

"Why's that hard to believe?"

"I didn't mean it like that. I just. I stole that kiss from you Clary. I'm sorry your first kiss was a stolen kiss. That makes me an asshole."

I turned all the way to him. "You're not an asshole. It was a dick move, maybe, and I said as much to Anna. But I'm actually really glad you stole that kiss. You made me feel desirable even when I thought it was a dare. No one has ever made me feel desired before you. There was passion in that kiss that you can't fake. I mean, just look at my painting." I gestured behind my shoulder, and Bryant grinned.

"Okay. Fair enough. I accept your answer."

"What about you?"

"What about me?" We moved slowly up the line again, but his main focus stayed on me.

"Tell me something about you."

"Oh, that's loaded." He said, then stroked his chin like I had. "Let's see. I do like peas, I'm not a big fan of carpet either, my favorite smell is strawberry, sort of like your shampoo, this is my suit, I own six of them."

The charm rolling off him as he parroted my answers entranced me. I couldn't believe he remembered so easily. "And something real?"

He thought on it for a moment. I could actually see him trying to decide what to say. It was his game, what made him so self-conscious? "I graduated in December. I chose not to go to spring semester at Huntsly right away like my parents expected me to. Instead, I got a crappy job and bought this car with my savings from birthdays and my first loan and started going to more of Annabelle's parties to blow off steam. I started taking more art classes and looking for shows like the fundraiser. I don't want to be a lawyer, or a doctor, or a psychiatrist like my parents have expected of me since I could walk. I'm eighteen. I don't know what I want to do. I'll figure it out in the fall, you know?"

I did. I knew about all of that exactly. Except, I had the luxury of enjoying my summer. It sounded like Bryant didn't. "Is that really what's expected of you? College and a high profile job?"

"Oh yeah. My dad is a cosmetic surgeon. He makes a lot of money with a lot of high profile people. He donates his time to helping disfigured children as well. And he's good at it. I'm supposed to find something I'm good at and continue the fortunes, but only if it's also high profile. Make him proud. My name published everywhere. But what if I want to paint? Or work with the hungry, or the ill, or the homeless? I love these fundraisers like tonight. All that money they raised for those kids. That's my passion."

"I think that's an extremely noble aspiration Bryant, and you should be proud of that despite what others expect of you."

"I had you on my arm all night, Clarissa. That makes me proud."

He pulled my hand into his lap as he tucked my elbow under his. He planted one soft kiss on my mouth and moved up in line. Two more cars left, and we turned the corner out of the driveway and back to the river's edge. Back to my neighborhood.

"You're different than I thought you were," I confessed.

"Is it the jokes? Because really humor is very selective." He grinned.

"No, seriously. I thought you were just another jerk who cared about physical attraction and keeping up appearances but you're not. Maybe you started off wrong, but you're deep, and you're a good person. I can tell."

"It was awkward," he said, then paused; the silence hung in the space between us. "I didn't know what to do when I felt that spark while I was watching you. So, I just kissed you. And then I felt like I was twelve again and couldn't figure out how to talk to you.

Hey thanks for not punching me even though I deserved it."

"Well thanks for not trying to kiss me again when I shoved you away."

He just winked at me and shifted the car again. We rode the rest of the way in a comfortable silence while his thumb rubbed circles on the side of my wrist, and my heart hammered the whole way.

Chapter Six

Bryant dropped me off at my door with a long, luxurious kiss on the porch. His hands wrapped in my hair on both sides of my face and he pulled me into him until I thought I would melt right through his surface.

Until the light flipped on overhead, and I knew it was time to come in.

"Ah yes. Alas, parting is such sweet sorrow," he recited with one last kiss on my hand and a promise to get in touch with me that week.

My mother ushered me and my painting inside, and we gossiped over tea about the events of the evening, sans my patio risqué, then she declared her exhaustion and went to bed.

I, on the other hand, laid on my bed for an hour with sleep nowhere in sight.

Ping.

Cross: I'm awake. It's an evening of nocturnal activity. Are you awake?

> Who can sleep on a night like this?

Cross: It's a shame there's so many miles between us. Next time I'll figure in something else to do after bedtime.

> Next time huh? You seem fairly confident there's more days between us.

Cross: Oh princess. You better believe there's a next time coming in swiftly. Gotta go little gazelle. Dream of me. X

***

I woke up late the next morning, surprised to find it was already ten AM. My parents left for work long before. I stayed up well past two thinking about what Bryant asked me the night before. *Something real, something that was only me.* I had so little that was only me.

I climbed out of bed and padded to my closet. Pulling it open, I dug through the hangers. I pulled out everything that actually belonged to Annabelle. There was a lot and what remained made the space look so vacant.

Half a dozen cardigans, the same amount of tank tops, a couple calf length skirts, and my sundress still hung on the bar. Dismal.

A trip to my dresser didn't reveal much else after I removed Annabelle's mini skirts and crop tops. All jeans and a handful of t-shirts and pullover sweaters.

This is who I was. I liked my jeans and sweaters, comfortable and not flashy. I didn't like to be flashy all the time. Anna liked to dress me up, but sometimes I preferred to be unnoticed. It's quieter. Easier. Safer.

I folded all of Anna's clothing into a neat pile and tucked it in a rolling case. We were leaving for school soon, she should go through all this anyway and see what would go with us.

I pulled on some jeans and a tank top and put a soft fabric headband in my chestnut hair to hold the top down before I tossed my flip flops on my feet.

Grabbing my keys, I pulled the door closed behind me. When I turned around to lock it, I noticed a neatly folded piece of paper taped to the door with my name on it.

I pulled it off and flipped it open:

9:30pm

1800 Rutherford Dr

Bring a sweater and your pretty self. Nothing else required.

-B

A date after bedtime. Swiftly requested as promised. Interesting. I tucked the note away, Annabelle would love to see this.

✷✷✷

"Oh my gosh! On the patio?!" Annabelle's eyes looked like they were going to bug all the way out of her head. "I was looking around for you guys but there were so many people, I didn't see you. Maybe you were

65

actually outside getting all freaky deaky." She waggled her eyebrows at me.

"I wouldn't call it freaky deaky. Just, heavy kissing? Making out?" I threw my head back. "Ugh, I don't know. But it was really, really great. And look." I passed her the note that was on my door.

"A secret rendezvous. How exciting. Hey, what are you going to wear? I have this cute jumpsuit that would be amazing on you." She was already beelining to her wardrobe.

"Anna, no. I'm going to just go casual. Be me, you know? See, it even says 'bring a sweater and yourself.' I'm just going to wear some leggings and a tank top and a cardigan probably."

"Ugh. Men don't know what they're talking about. This would look totally adorable. It'll make you scrumptious." She swung a burgundy one piece at me with a plunging neckline sing-songing the whole time.

"Thanks, Anna, but really, I'm good." I pasted on the most sincere smile I could muster. "We can save that one for date number three." I told her with a wink. She pouted but seemed appeased; she put the jumpsuit away and plopped back down on the bed on her stomach, her feet kicked up behind her..

"Okay. So, then tell me about the suitcase you rolled in here."

"Oh!" I jumped up. "This is all your clothes out of my room!"

"Clarissa Monroe! Are you breaking up with me?" She looked genuinely horrified as her mouth dropped open and her eyebrows rose on her forehead.

"What? No way! I just figured if we're leaving for school soon, maybe you want to sort stuff out? I need to do the same. And figure out what's mine."

"It's all yours too. I love you, boo. We're staying together, so you could've brought it all with." She dug through the bag. "And this? This top looks a million times better on you than me, it was never really mine. You have that super long, slender torso. You keep it, it belongs to you now, you're its mommy."

I wondered in that moment why Anna really dressed me up. Was it a reflection on what she felt for herself? I opted to let her give me back everything she thought belonged on me, which was more than half of what I brought back, and most of it I would disagree with. Even though I knew I wanted to try to be more of myself again, she seemed so happy in that moment that I couldn't tell her no again. Anna was a part of me too.

When she pulled out a beautiful soft cream half-button sweater though, I decided I could say yes to those hopeful eyes twinkling at me and wear it tonight. Because this one did look really great on me, and it was warm.

"Knock 'em dead kid." She giggled as I shrugged the sweater on and plunged back into her excitement over our big move.

***

I pulled onto Rutherford Drive trying again to figure out where I could possibly be meeting Bryant. This section of town was mostly old plantation houses and many of them were abandoned. House 1800 would be most the way down the long, dark street with several of the street lamps burnt out along the way.

Pulling into 1800, I could see I was in for a winding drive. This was one of the longer driveways at the end of the block, and beyond this street was mostly forest until you hit the river. I didn't get far before old carriage lamps lit my way. Most looked like originals that had been there for ages, but some of the others glowed a faint lavender color. Bryant.

Further down the drive, as the trees thickened, small glowing globes hanging from the branches accompanied the carriage lamps. The effect was a twinkling fairyland look. It was so pretty against the encroaching darkness. I cruised through the rest of the drive and at the end stood Crossman, one more lavender lantern in hand.

I parked my car, and he opened the door. "I'm so glad you came." He swooped in for a brief kiss.

"I am too, what a beautiful drive in. The lights in the trees are amazing."

"It is a nice touch. I love this driveway. I had to brighten it up for you a bit since you don't know the way, but it really is a beautiful entrance. You should see it in the daylight sometime. There's lots of landscaping inside the tree line." He laced his fingers with mine and pulled me along the path.

"Where are we going? Isn't this private property? We aren't going to get in trouble are we?"

Bryant gave a short laugh and shook his head. "One of my dads clients owns this house, but they're only here in the fall usually, and since the house had been undergoing repairs, they haven't been back in a few years. But, we have permission to come out to the grounds whenever we'd like. It's one of my favorite places. I've been coming here since I was a kid. It's okay Clary, I'm not that much of a bad boy that I'd risk sending you to jail, and I'm not a murderer. If you ever need someone's house TP'd that did you wrong though? Count me in."

"People still TP houses?"

"When they do their girl wrong? Absolutely," he said with a wink.

"Your girl huh? Is that what I am now? 'Cross's girl'?"

"Only if you want to be." He stopped us, a question in his eyes. It was undeniable the answer he sought, plain in his pleading gaze as he gently squeezed my hand.

"I think I'd like that." No sooner had I finished my answer was I rewarded with another kiss. This one longer, faster, and fiercer. Bryant had made himself vulnerable for a moment, and the nervous energy poured out of him, smoothing away to relief and hunger.

"You're like a magnet. Come on, we need to keep moving before I get sucked in again." He pulled me forward with his free hand, and we walked through a path of topiaries.

When we cleared the other side it opened up to a beautiful side pond. Small lanterns were spaced every ten feet or so along the water's edge. They were mirrored and reflected back in another line. A blanket lay before us with a small spread of fruit and breads. A bottle rested in an ice bucket with two fancy plastic cups beside it.

"What's this?" I asked, half excited and half bewildered.

"There's a meteor shower tonight. Do you like stars? I thought we could watch and see if we see anything and enjoy an evening picnic. The bottle is sparkling cider, don't worry. We're both driving. So. Yeah. Safety."

I stepped forward into the space and found a seat on the blanket. I looked over the water in wonder. I could view the brilliance of the constellations in the reflection with the lights. The pond was still and beautiful and the sky was clear and bright with stars. The reflection twinkled back at me, a thousand tiny lights dancing across its glass surface. "This is incredible."

"I hoped you would like it." One hand was stuffed in his pocket and the other was on the back of his neck. It was sweet and adorable at the same time. He was nervous, it was almost puzzling against his usual demeanor. Bryant Crossman always seemed cool and confident and easy.

"So. You're an art buff, you only drink sometimes, and you're into the stars? Everyone pegs you for the nonchalant, wild, rich kid but you, Mr. Crossman? Well, I suspect you're sort of nerdy on the inside."

He laughed and moved to sit beside me. He grabbed the cups and poured us each a glass of sparkling cider then took a long drink before replying. "You would be sort of right. I play both ends. I hate that people think you have to be one thing or another. You can be wild and carefree and the life of the party and still enjoy things people call, what did you just call me? *Nerdy*?" Amusement twinkled in his eyes. "I thought nerdy people called other nerdy people 'intellectual'."

"Only to other not nerds. We know we're nerds, but it's our little secret."

"Well then, I guess I've joined the nerd club. Is there a secret handshake too? A hazing? Do I need to get a special haircut?" He quirked a brow at the last inquiry, and I couldn't help it, I burst out laughing.

"No, no. You just have to be kind and take no shit. In private though. Bullies are scary."

"I bet they are. So, Clary. Tell me all about your nerdom while I try to figure out which side of the sky we're supposed to be able to see this thing in." The moonlight soaked into his face and distracted me for a moment with the way it dotted his light hair and sloped over his nose to light up just the edges of his lips. Bryant was beautiful, and he looked so at home under the stars.

"I don't really know. I've just always found the typical teenage things over blown. Other kids were always talking about the latest episode of some reality show, and I was watching classic cartoons and old Hollywood movies. The girls would be grinding to hip hop, and I was lost in classical piano. I'll pick up classic literature over a magazine any day and pretty soon people started calling me a nerd." I shrugged. "My grandma called it the curse of an old soul. Maybe I'm just an old lady stuck in this teenage body."

Bryant threw me a lopsided grin and looked me up and down. "Well if there's an old lady here somewhere, you sure do cover her well. I think it's great you're different. Why be like everyone else when you can blossom into something undiscovered?"

"Undiscovered to whom? Are you saying I'm a conquest?"

His eyes bore into mine with an abrupt intensity as he moved closer. "Never. What I'm saying, Clary, is that I think there's someone deep down inside you that even you don't know exists because you've never found her." He tucked a stray curl behind my ear and paused. "I think when you do, you're going to bloom into something truly magical and completely your own. And I hope I'm here to see it."

I was lost in his eyes. I closed mine for a brief moment, savoring his touch just behind my ear. The small circles he rubbed on my scalp while he watched me warmed my insides. "It's weird how you can see what I feel when everyone else thinks they have me figured out. I've never felt like I was living the true me. I wish I could pull her out. I feel like she's daring, and ready to explore the world, and herself, and she's carefree. But I'm the one on the outside because she doesn't know how to break through, stuck in there by the expectations of what a good girl should be. You know?"

Bryant watched me intently, quiet, hand still behind my ear; his thumb on my jaw stroked me lightly before speaking. "Maybe she just needs someone to coax her out and show her it's safe." He leaned forward and kissed me gently then kissed my forehead.

"What do you say we watch for these stars?" he asked as he handed me a pile of grapes, "and have a late night snack?"

He picked up his phone and searched the sky with it, pointing out constellations between bites of brie and jam. His face was animated. Bright in a way that you don't see on most people day to day. This was his element. This quiet, dark space with only the sky and soft lanterns showing us one another and our delightful treat. I couldn't help but study this part of him. I had a feeling he didn't give it away often. It made me reflect on what we said. Was there some of that in me as well? What wasn't I bringing to the surface?

The first meteor falling through the sky excited us. Our exclamations rang out over the water, and we both dropped our food back into the basket. Bryant laid on the blanket, and I laid on his outstretched arm. The star's brightness intensified as another meteor rushed across our vision.

"I've never seen a shooting star," I said. "It's so much more beautiful than I would've imagined."

"You probably can't see them in town, especially down by you, it's too bright. You need to be out in the dark like this. When I was a kid my dad took us out on the boat one summer to watch a meteor shower. So, there we were off the coast of the Atlantic, and the sky lights up. I'll never forget that night. Counting the meteors and looking out over the water. It was hypnotic, and so peaceful. I never thought much about the stars before then."

I turned on my side to watch him. He was so far away, in a totally different place from me at this moment. "You don't go out on the boat with him to do this sort of stuff anymore?"

He let out a hurt laugh and turned his face away slightly. "No. No, we don't. We don't do much of anything anymore. He's either at the office or out of town. Sometimes, I think he only tolerates us because he needs to. All he keeps talking about is me leaving for school soon and making something of myself. When am I leaving for school and what's my major? Which school did I pick? My mom always looks worried when he starts asking that. Where? How far away?"

It was vulnerable Bryant again, and I did the only thing I could think to do. I wrapped my arms around him and looked back up at the sky. "Tell me about that constellation."

He found my eyes then followed my hand, some tension released from his body as he told me about Bootes and the flock. We stayed that way long past the last of the falling stars, wishing on each one for a little more darkness.

Chapter Seven

I woke up to something wet on my cheek with air puffing in my ear. I jolted up and leapt back with a cry.

But there, sitting where I had been, was a small beagle sniffing around again. He lapped up whatever crumbs he found and scratched his ear with a little bark.

"Ah, you've met Duncan. He sort of roams wherever he pleases," Bryant said as he emerged from the pathway leading into our picnic space.

"Yeah, I see that. I thought no one lived here right now?" I rubbed the goober off my face.

"He's the groundskeepers. She comes a few times a week to take care of the grass and plants, and

Duncan comes along. Cute little guy when he wants to play. Sort of a slobber monster when you've slept in food. Not that I do that often." Bryant ruffled Duncan's ears and handed me a cup. "Coffee. You are human and drink coffee, right? I added cream, it seemed like it might be your style."

"Coffee, yes. Human in the morning, debatable."

He laughed as I rummaged through the basket looking for anything that might pass for sweet. Finding a tube of honey I decided if it was good enough for tea, it's good enough for coffee. I stirred it with my finger and took a huge gulp.

"That's an interesting combination. Need a little sweet with your bitter?"

"Forever," I grumped.

"You're not a morning person." Bryant pointed at me, a statement and not a question. That devilish grin back on his face. "I'll just tuck that tidbit away."

I couldn't help but laugh. "You use that phrase enough that I'm noticing it."

"Ah. Yes. My grandma used to say that. I guess I sort of picked it up. But it hasn't failed me yet. I remember everything I tuck away." He tapped his temple and planted a sweet kiss on my nose before he stood and offered me his hand. "Let's go inside for a few minutes. That's where you'll find another cup of coffee and a bathroom." He smiled down at my now empty cup and pulled me to my feet; then scooped up the blanket and the basket in one swoop. With a little adjusting and a skip over Duncan we were off. Hand in hand up the path to the house.

Coming through in the dark last night, I missed the sweeping landscape behind the house and the stunning paths of flowers leading to it. They blended into a beautiful mosaic of lilac, pink, and white set against cream colored stone paths with small garden lamps lining the pathways.

"These gardens are really beautiful. It's a shame they're not being enjoyed."

"Oh but they are. They're so beautiful because Cheryl works so hard on them. She loves being out here. It's not just a job for her." His eyes looked joyful.

"It's part of the reason they hired her. Because being passionate about your gardens in a way that really makes you happy makes for a more beautiful spread."

I glanced at him and he held up the hand that was attached to mine.

"Her words. I'm not a gardener."

"I suppose the same could be true about painting. Being passionate about your canvas in a way that really makes you happy makes for a more beautiful painting."

"That's true. But painting isn't only about passion. You have to believe what the canvas makes you feel. You can feel what you're painting all you want, but if you don't believe it. Well. That's why so many beautiful paintings are so sad when the subject matter should be happy. Because your viewer sees what you believe, not necessarily what you want them to feel." He stopped just shy of the door and turned to me. "It's just like what people try to portray outwardly. You can try to make people see something you're putting out. But if you don't believe it, they can't either." And then he stepped inside.

***

Bryant claimed we were making a pit stop on the way home then pulled into The Havens, my grandmother's shelter. She waved from the entryway, and I got out of my car and rapped on Bryant's window.

"Pit stop? What are we doing?"

"Well, I talked to your dad who told me where this place was. He said your grandma might need a hand today with birthday parties. It seemed like a fun day to help with." He beamed at me from his seat looking young and innocent and clearly pleased with himself.

"Your funeral," I laughed as he opened the door.

"Aw it can't be that bad. Cake, ice cream, musical chairs?" He wound his arms around my waist and pulled me in tight.

"Oh, I'm definitely going to enjoy watching this. It's always chaos if they sugar up before play time, or long bouts of game rematches. Ever played Candyland for three hours straight?" I stood on my tiptoes to press a quick kiss to his cheek and grabbed his hand; I eagerly towed him into the shelter past my grandma who winked at me.

We walked into the party room to find most of the kids already there playing board games and drinking punch. A loud buzzing filtered throughout the small, sunlit room while parents and kids chattered on with one another. The shelter celebrated everyone's birthday once a month, kids and adults alike, so there was always a lot of energy as kids anticipated the party's arrival day. I led Bryant to the reading corner and deposited him in a giant bean bag chair and sat in the one next to him.

A little girl stood at the shelves, she had turned and focused on Bryant. She couldn't have been much more than four years old and kept peeking over with curiosity. After a few minutes, her decision made, she wandered over to us with a small stack of books balanced in her hands. Spreading the books out at Bryant's feet, she pondered over them before picking one about foxes and looking into Bryant's face.

"What do you have there?" he asked. "Can I see?"

The girl nodded and held the book out proudly in front of her. Her lips were upturned and her nose was scrunched up while she beamed at him. Bryant plucked the book from her fingers and looked at the cover.

"Oh! *Fox's Fall Day*. That sounds like a fun story. Do you like foxes?" he asked. She nodded and smiled at him again before crawling in his lap and turning around to face the book.

Bryant looked up at me, surprised, and I shrugged. "It looks like it's story time Mr. Crossman," I said with a smile. I stood, moving to the door to take in the scene.

As Bryant opened the book and started to read, several more of the younger kids joined them on the soft reading corner carpet to listen to the story.

"It looks like your friend found some more friends," my grandma said, coming up beside me, her hand soft and soothing on my back.

"It does look that way, doesn't it?"

"They don't see a lot of men," she said, "Most of them have no positive male in their lives, and they can all sense the good in people. It's rare to get a volunteer like him here these days."

I nodded, and we stood listening as Bryant finished the story. He closed the book and another child thrust a new choice at him with a chorus of "please" sounding among the kids. Bryant smiled and ruffled a few heads before opening the next book and reading with enthusiasm. The kids listened patiently, completely focused on the same man I watched and saw in a different light. Another joined his lap after the second book, thrusting a third at him to start again.

Bryant read six stories before it was time for cake and gifts. He walked to me with a huff, chugging water. We sang happy birthday with big enthusiasm; Bryant whooped at the end as the kids worked together to blow out candles. He hurried over to help my grandma serve, seeming to be inside an element that excited him.

When presents were done and kids were corralled after an explosion of energy, we helped with a quick clean up before going home. Bryant beamed ear to ear the whole time we tidied and as we walked to the front door he turned and returned to my grandma's side. He grabbed her hands and swung them out as he relayed his joy in the afternoon we spent. He asked her if he could come back and she nodded at him enthusiastically, her eyes glistening with unshed tears with the kind words he left her with. Their exchange made my heart swell.

Chapter Eight

Shopping. *Ugh.*

Anna happily skipped along beside me talking my ear off about all the amazing things I should buy for the day trip Bryant invited me on two days prior. The butt crack of dawn coffee and scones at some adorable boardwalk he thought I'd like as we watched the sun come up before leaving town day trip. The rest was a mystery but I knew one thing; It should be illegal to be up before the sun.

I was informed, however, that the trip required a bathing suit. Thus, the shopping. Because while most of Anna's clothes did fit me, anything resembling undergarments would not work. You could fit both of my boobs in one of her bra cups with room to spare.

Shopping. *Ugh.*

"He really told you absolutely nothing? If you have to be up that early to get a start so you can be home by curfew it must be something exciting. How far do you think you'll be driving? Oh! What about that amusement park up north with the splash coasters? That's like, three hours away, do you think it's that? Wouldn't that be awesome?"

"Dear heavens, I hope not. Splash coasters? That sounds nauseating."

"Yeah. But you can scream and grab his arm. Pretend to be afraid and get all cozy." She bounced a little while I laughed.

"Somehow, I don't think I would have to pretend."

"Aw, come on, Clary! Where's your sense of thrill? If it's not something daring then what do you think it is?"

I thought back to our conversations over the last week. Of the stars, of cottages nestled deep in the woods, of dreams of hot air balloons high up in the clouds and the wind wrapping around us like a cold caress, total freedom from everything down below found high up in the sky. Talks of places to travel and things to see and dreams to fulfill and utter freedom. But nothing with a swimsuit.

"Well, it's not a hot air balloon."

Anna's eyebrows pressed together. "It's not what?"

"Never mind. Maybe he got invited to a cookout at the lake or something and wanted to go there but also wanted to see me. Easy win win. Now, let's find this suit and get out of here."

"Oh! If you're going to meet his friends, you need a new top! Not a crop top because, hello, swimming! That totally requires a tube top! I saw a super cute fuchsia one yesterday when I was here, we could," she froze mid-sentence when she finally realized I stopped walking, two sentences ago. "What?"

"No crop tops, no tube tops, no mini skirts."

"Um, okaaay. You'd look so cute though!"

"I just want to feel like me, Annabelle. I love hanging out with you and feeling all glamorous. But it's like an all day date. And if I am meeting his friends or whatever, you're not there. I can't be comfortable like that without you. I need to feel like me." I side eyed a rack while Anna tried to find words. I was stunned I had successfully stunned her into silence. "What about this?" I picked up a lavender tank top off a table. The front had a v-cut of black lace that ran into the sleeves where it disappeared into the hem. It was slightly acid washed in a way that almost looked marbled. I grabbed a black circle skirt hanging on a rack behind it. "And this?"

Anna eyed the pairing, her eyes bounced between my face and the outfit in my hands. "Lavender? I've never seen you in lavender. But that lace is edgy. At least it's not mom jeans," she said with a head tilt. "Well, come on, you know where the fitting rooms are. I'll find you a mom suit." She waved me off as she walked away, and I turned for the fitting rooms.

Closing myself into a room, I let out a sigh and tried on the outfit. When I saw myself in the big mirror outside the dressing room, I couldn't help but wonder who I picked the tank for. Myself, or Anna. It didn't matter, because the second I laid eyes on myself and did a little twirl in the knee length skirt, watching it kick up and spin around with me like an extension of myself, I knew. I knew it was my freedom peeking out, readying itself to carry me away.

Anna came in moments later carrying the tiniest red one piece suit with side cut outs and practically no back. "Hear me out. Didn't find a mom suit, did find this little stunner. One piece, because it's you. Red, because *hello*. If he takes you to a pool or a lake you need to be able to be seen in the water since you fall on air and also because red is totally your color even though you hate it because it draws attention. BTW it draws attention because you're a total babe, you just refuse to realize it. And cut outs because it's as close as I'm going to get to you showing off any part of the front of yourself, but this back." She let out a whistle and her eyes twinkled. "This back is sexy babe, and with the way you said he was toying with that plunge in the blue dress at the fundraiser. Girl you most definitely need an open back swimsuit. Trust me."

I didn't even bother trying it on. If I put that thing on before I needed to be in it, I would put it back. And that wasn't going to be an option. I took Anna's word for it.

A few hours later, my phone dinged as I settled into bed. My stomach fluttered like it could read the screen without my eyes.

Cross: How goes it, sleepy gazelle?

How did this man always know it was my bedtime? Every day since we started talking on the phone he always messaged right at bedtime. Maybe Anna was right, maybe I am predictable. But at least it gave me room for a conversation.

Just getting snuggled in.

Cross: Snuggled huh? Does that involve a body pillow I should be jealous of? A stuffed animal? Not another boyfriend right?

Bryant always knew how to bubble a laugh out of me. It's like I was wrong and he *could* read me like a book, despite my telling him I wasn't one. Heavy moments were always soothed with laughter; it seemed so easy for him.

Are you jealous of stuffing? What if I told you it was just a pile of blankets? Wrapped around me like a burrito.

Cross: I'd say the blankets were getting the best deal.

How's that?

Three dots bounced on the screen then stopped, then bounced. Again, and again and finally a new message popped in.

Cross: Because they get to wrap
around you, caress your ass while
they hug your breasts, touch all the
places I can conjure up in my mind
but can't touch with my hands. Like
a whisper across your thighs when
you move, sliding across your stomach
to touch your hips, brush across your
nipples as you roll to the other side.
Are you wearing pajamas, or are you
naked? Do you feel the brush of your
blankets when your nipples harden,
gazelle?

My mouth went dry. His words plowed through me, lighting me up inside. I felt tight and hot in *so* many places.

**A pink satin nightgown.
It's so soft.**

My phone buzzed in my hand, and the top of the screen showed: Cross. I punched the answer button, but he spoke before I could even say hello, "Now I'm jealous of your nighty. Slip down the straps princess and stand up, let it glide down your body."

"What are we doing?" I ask him.

"Whatever feels right. I've been stuck all day on that image of you against the wall in that wicked blue dress with your thigh up over me. I couldn't not message you, and now I can't stop thinking about the sound that nighty would make as it hits the floor." His voice was like melted butter, slick and thick and dangerous.

I stood.

Swallowing and still holding the phone, I slid one strap off my shoulder. My breath shuddered through me as I slid the other one over the edge and down my arm. I switched the phone to the other side to release the strap, so I could still hear Bryant's unsteady breathing as the silk slid down my body and hit the floor.

My uncontrollable moan, as the fabric did exactly what he said it would and slipped over my pebbled nipples, was barely audible but followed by one of Bryant's own.

"Good girl," he croaked. "Now follow the trail with your fingertips, tell me what you feel."

"I feel like my skin is full of electricity," I tell him as I drift the backs of my fingers over my arm and down my side, brushing the underside of my breast and dipping over my hip. "It jumps like it's alive and I feel tingles every time I touch my own skin."

I breathe out a sigh which he repeats back through the phone before he tells me to climb into bed. A little nervous but feeling exhilarated about the simple things I've done I get back in bed and cover up to my ears.

"What are you thinking, Clary?" My name in his husky voice sent shivers down my spine.

"I'm wondering what's happening on the other side of this call, and what my hands would feel like if they were yours."

"Are you? Put your hands where you want mine. Tell me how you like to touch yourself when you think about my mouth on yours, my hands in your hair and on your body, my hips pinning you in place with your legs open to me. What does it do to you, Clary? To know that you make me wild. Does it make you feel powerful?"

I flush with heat he can't even see.

Pressing the blankets back a fraction, I slid one hand down and tentatively dragged my fingers from one hip bone to the other, pulling them back to the center and brushing into my curls. I've touched myself many times, but never with an audience even if he is only on the phone. I pressed a finger through and swirled my clit, dipping my fingers into my moisture and bringing it back to swirl again. A light moan escaped me and I heard Bryant hiss on the other end.

"That is the sexiest sound. Tell me what makes you make that sound."

I hesitated, and it only took him a split second to react again.

He cleared his throat."It's okay if you're not okay. I can bid you goodnight, and we can go to sleep. I know things are new, and you don't know me well and, well—"

His fumbling words embolden me, and I almost don't recognize the airy voice that comes out when I say, "I'm pressing on my clit with my wetness. One finger dipped in to make it wet then slow circles. I like to draw it out." I for sure think that sounds so ridiculous since I have no idea how to talk sexy to someone when I hear Bryant drop a low, drawn out f-bomb through the line.

"Keep going," he cajoles, "press a little harder and make it fast for me."

I obliged, intrigued by the uptick in the pace of his breathing, the little hiccups I heard became more frequent and I panted through on my own side.

"Oh, good girl. Now, put your middle finger inside and rub with your thumb instead."

I never played that way but scooted up a bit to reach the requested finger into my wet heat and twist my thumb around to apply pressure back to my aching clit. The pleasure was almost too much and I fumbled the phone in my grip. "Oh Bryant, oh my goodness, I,"

"I know." He replied as he cooed words at me I couldn't make out between his pants and my own breathy moans. "Come for me baby, let's finish together. Use your other finger to pinch with your thumb, pinch and rub and make it good since I can't feel you myself."

I barely made it through the end of his sentence before I cried out and tumbled over the edge of bliss. A choked cry echoes from the other side of the phone followed by another low moan that rippled through me like the hum of the bass on the dance floor.

And then a knock on my door followed by my mother's voice startled me, "Clary, is everything okay? I thought I heard something."

I slapped my hand over my mouth to hide my giggles as Bryant's chuckle came over the line. "Fine mom! Go to bed. Good night!"

"Well, okay, but if you need something. Good night."

I put the phone to my ear as Bryant sighed. "Well that's one way to get out of having to figure out what to say next. Are you satisfied, gazelle? Because I am thoroughly satisfied."

Sometimes, Bryant Crossman on the other side of the phone, or the other side of the car, or calling me pet names, still felt like a dream. And this is one of those times, I thought. In a too soft voice, I said, "So satisfied. The only thing that could top that is if it were your hand instead of mine.”

“Next time,” he replied. “Definitely next time. I’ll talk to you in the morning, Clary. Sleep sweet princess.”

The call clicked off. My phone chimed with an image of a sleepy, hair mussed, shirtless Bryant smiling at me. I clicked my own headshot before I dove into the depths of the blankets and fell asleep almost instantly with his promise of next time still ringing in my ears.

Chapter Nine

Another week with Annabelle breezed by with talks of what would go to the dorms with us, sorting her clothes, again, and late nights with our favorite movies and big buckets of popcorn until we passed out on the foot of her bed with the screen still going. When I was at home in my relative quiet compared to Anna's stream of constant noise and music, I was generally on the other side of a call with Bryant, engrossed in deep conversation. He reminded me of myself in so many ways, complete with a gentle spirit and a love for all things.

It was after one of those late nights, with no questions answered about our early morning date the next day that I woke up to a gentle, steady *pat pat pat* on my window. I cracked my eyes open to the still dark. And rain.

Uh-oh Mr Crossman, it's raining.

Cross: No worries, unless you have somewhere to be tomorrow.

IDK what that means. What does that mean?

Cross: Well, the rain won't spoil our date, it'll just take us longer to get to the main event. Pack an overnight bag?

Overnight bag? The thought thrilled me, but there's no way that would fly.

My parents will never go for that.

Cross: Clary, you're 18 years old. You might live with them because you haven't moved to your dorm yet, and I will never, ever suggest that you disrespect them because that's wrong. But you're 18. If you still want to come with me, come. We can reschedule this to tomorrow, or we can ride out the rain tonight and get a beautiful morning view. Spread those wings and let them sail you to your freedom.

I worried my lip as I stared at the screen. I wasn't really sure why asking permission still felt so necessary, but he was right. It was my last summer, I didn't plan to ever come back like so many others did. Not without a really, really good reason, and I didn't see that reason ever coming to fruition. Why do I still feel like I need my parents to approve my every move?

An hour later, I walked over the boardwalk with a giant hot pink umbrella in one hand and an overnight bag in the other. My mom gave me a little fuss about real world dangers and not knowing if I should go overnight somewhere without knowing where I was going. But I promised her I'd message her, that I was absolutely safe with Bryant, and I would let her know where we ended up. Or at least I hoped I'd get to keep that promise. "Bring sneakers" and "beautiful morning view" could mean I'd end up in the mountains somewhere in a cabin with no reception for all I knew.

Contemplation aside I had to admit I was thrilled.

As my feet splashed along the wooden planks and the ocean sloshed lazily to my right, my eyes zeroed in on a tall, sandy haired thrill ride of a man under an awning ahead of me. Bryant not only proved to be tender and sweet and sensitive, but also naughty where I once thought he was simply wild and full of big world plans and dreams. My pulse spiked and my stomach fluttered as I came almost toe to toe with him.

"Well good morning gazelle." He smirked while dropping a kiss to my nose. His smirk turned to a full on kid-in-a-candy-store grin as he waved a cup of coffee under my nose and watched my excitement. "Heavy on the cream, and I used actual sugar, sugar."

"Ugh, you're perfect," I exclaimed before downing a huge gulp of the creamy sweetness of wake the hell up. "So, I presume we aren't standing around here being drowned all morning, right?"

"One hundred percent correct Miss Monroe. But before I can steer you one way or the other, I have to know the answer to the ultimate question."

"Which is?" I raised my eyebrows, more mystery. What a way to start my Saturday. Though, I suppose, I started that by sneaking out the front door while my mom baked whatever it was she and my dad ate for breakfast solo, so I didn't have to endure the wrath that was my dad after my mom inevitably spilled my plans.

"Pancakes, or waffles?" Bryant snapped my attention back to his megawatt smile.

"I could no sooner pick a favorite book. That's evil."

He erupted in laughter. "Okay, Central Market it is."

"Central Market? Now I've never been there because it's in the heart of uptown, but isn't that like, all sandwiches and rice bowls and kale salads and stuff?"

"Ah sweet, sweet Clary, the things you must learn. Central Market for the regular public? All those things. But when you know things, and I know things, every vendor will serve you breakfast before open, any breakfast you want, including a giant platter of pancakes and waffle sandwiches, complete with rolled chocolate crepes and beignets you can dip in the most rich caramel sauce you've ever tasted and fruit, of course. Just gotta know the password." He said with a tap on his temple.

"So it's like a key party but with food?" I was seriously missing out.

"Yeah, sort of, I suppose. Come on, it won't be busy yet. Rich kids don't get out of bed on a Saturday for a few more hours. Only the nerdy ones are up," he said with a wink and a tug on my hand. I followed behind sipping my coffee, light on my feet. Quite the Saturday indeed.

***

Much to my disappointment, we didn't enter Central Market with a key, or a pocket watch, or a special handshake. We entered it after Bryant knocked on a door and a very enthusiastic woman, with pale blue hair in the cutest pixie cut and a matching pixie dress, opened it. She turned on a smile as bright as the sun before she shouted Bryant's name and engulfed him in a hug. It was quite the spectacle but not unheard of, I was told. I had the pleasure of watching it happen again a few minutes later as we scoped out who had breakfast.

Central Market was a huge warehouse style building packed with what would probably be considered food trucks if they were on wheels. Each was elaborately laid out into a restaurant worthy ordering counter, reflective of the full sized spaces they represented. The menus were all plastered on the walls in so many different styles, some elegantly printed and framed, and others written on chalkboards or white boards by hand. But no breakfast menus. To find those, we had to walk past each restaurant and chat up whoever was getting the grills ready. Bryant said it's a solid way to connect with vendors. My stomach just rumbled.

In the end we got pancakes from one place, rolled crepes from another and waffle sandwiches, just as Bryant said. Each spot popped them all on a large tray the first owner materialized from under the counter. The smell was amazing. Caramel coffee enveloped a rich undertone of cinnamon and chocolate, each vendor we passed adding a new layer of warmth to the air wafting around us. I couldn't wait to dive into it.

Bryant set my plate in front of me and I poured syrupy sweetness over the whole of it. Maple ran over chocolate bits in the pancakes and crepes making everything glimmer in stickiness. I moaned as I took the first bite of the melded flavors. Feeling his gaze on me, I peeked up. Clear amusement shone in Bryant's eyes as he watched me pop another huge bite of crepes in my mouth. Whip cream lined my upper lip. "See something amusing, Crossman?"

"No, I see something adorable. You're so expressive, and you're devouring something that clearly pleases you. I think it's cute and beyond sexy watching your face." His head quirked to the left, "And I think I want some." He surprised me by leaning over the table and pulling my upper lip into his mouth, after a small swipe of his tongue he released my lip with an audible popping noise and returned to his seat with an appreciative groan. "So much sweeter off your mouth. Ugh. Fuck it."

No sooner had the words left his mouth he jumped out of his seat, only to grab the one next to me and yank me into his lap. My lips crashed into his. My chest connected with his hard pecs and knocked the air from my lungs. His tongue lined the seam of my mouth and begged me to open.

I broke contact for a moment to gulp in fresh air; it was all the invitation Bryant needed to fuse his mouth on mine, and his tongue swept inside. Hazy lust filled my unexpecting mind as his hands swept into my hair and pulled me even closer to him. He tilted my chin up at the same time, so he could adjust his angle and deepen the kiss.

His intake of breath was audible when I wiggled to pull my feet up on the side of the chair, so I had something to balance on. He went completely still for a moment then, with a growl deep in his throat, tightened the hold on my hair and thrust up. It was my turn to gasp as I turned crimson red, and my eyes sprang open. I found Bryant staring at me with dilated pupils.

"Perhaps we should move outside the public's eye, and off each other's laps" He drawled out, sneaked a peek into his and then to a nearby table whispering to one another over our spectacle.

"That. Yes, that might be good." I couldn't think beyond what he suggested, and it took us another moment to come apart. Bryant scooped me off his lap and set me on my feet, steadying me with a hand on my hip and kissed my hand before letting go.

He quickly and quietly packed up the rest of our breakfast and handed me my coffee to finish with a kiss on the cheek. Pixie girl gave us a wave as we moved past her through the door and sent me a wink as Bryant popped a crisp twenty dollar bill in a communal tip jar, and then we stepped outside in the rain once more. Bryant dragged open my umbrella and held it over me.

"Where to?" I asked.

"Well Miss Monroe, since you've been so patient as to not ask me all the way through coffee and breakfast, I'll tell you. We're headed to the marina."

"The marina? You've got to be kidding me."

"Nope." Bryant smiled with mischief clear in his eyes. "Ever been on the ocean when the whales are headed to Canada for the season? It's incredible. I keep missing it because I've been sent off to some posh summer program or another every year kicking and screaming the whole way. But after our summer plans chat the other night, I decided that I'd unenroll myself for this year since I can, and go watch the damn whales because it's what I want to do. My dad wasn't happy when the director called him, but he'll get over it." He produced a set of keys from his pocket and dangled them from his middle finger; they swung softly back and forth. "So, I grabbed the keys to the boat, kissed my mother goodbye and left without a word. It's all ours for the night. What do you say? Wanna go watch some whales? Expand that sense of adventure you're trying to find?"

"I think I say, which boat do those keys belong to?"

Bryant did a giddy little jump, let out a whoop, and tugged me along down the dock by my hand as fast as the wet planks would allow.

We stopped just in front of a beautiful blue and white cruising yacht. It looked sharp and fast and a little dangerous with its pointed nose and railings. The upper deck was adorned with swanky looking lounge furniture, and a mermaid flag lazily swayed on the roof. "A mermaid?" I asked.

"Her name is the Sea Nymph. My dad has always been intrigued by the beautiful women of the sea. I told you, cosmetic surgeon. He doesn't do all his jobs to help people, he's obsessed with beauty and sex appeal. But she's a pretty boat, she deserves the name."

"Makes sense. So, Captain, can we climb aboard? You can drive this thing, right?"

"Ouch!" Bryant slapped a hand to his very wet chest and feigned injury. "You pain me so. Of course I can drive this thing. I practically breathe ocean water, might as well be a merman." He hopped up on the deck as he finished his sentence and held out a hand. "Gotta ditch the umbrella though. You're going to need the other hand to get up."

His eyes lit on a twinkle as my mouth dropped, and I folded the umbrella. I tucked it in the bag slung over my elbow and took his still outstretched hand. I held the handle of the railing with the other hand and brought my foot up. I wobbled and tumbled into

Bryant who expected it; he held firm with a laugh. His breath was hot on my wet cheek, and he tucked a piece of hair behind my ear that clung to my neck and over my lip.

"This is gorgeous. All these drenched curls, they're incredible." Both hands dipped in my hair as he brought my lips to his then let go just as quickly to grab my hand and tow me toward the cabin. "Let's get dry," he said with a quick smile as we ducked inside.

We walked quickly through a lounge, past a mini kitchen and into a bathroom definitely not large enough for the both of us. Bryant passed me a towel out of the cabinet. He shucked off his shirt and tossed it in the stand up shower and shook like a dog; water flew everywhere.

I giggled as his shorts followed his flash of a smile and he planted a quick kiss on my cheek. "I'm going to go make something warm to drink. But first I'll be back with some dry clothes. Chuck your wet ones in the shower with mine and dry off. There's a dryer on the lower deck, I'll throw it all in when you're changed. Toss the stuff in your overnight bag in there too if it's wet. I'll be back in one sec." He walked out of the room and clicked the door closed behind him.

I stood there bewildered at how easily he stripped and walked away.

Chapter Ten

An hour later we found ourselves curled into a lounge couch sipping Earl Grey tea and dissecting our favorite playlists.

"Rainy day?" Bryant asked.

"What? Like this never ending pounding on the side of this boat I let you drag me on?" I asked with a laugh, eyebrows high. "That's easy. The Neighborhood."

"Oh, intrigue! How do you get to them? Isn't that like, super upbeat? I would've figured you for a sappy slow artist like Jewel or something for rainy days."

"Rain needs happiness. Besides, rain *is* happiness. The smell is so clean, the sound is soothing. When it's over everything is fresh and new again. The birds sing more loudly, the animals all come out to scavenge. It's so refreshing. But anyway, The Neighborhood is like the ultimate background music. It feeds off whatever is happening. It sounds uppy, but they're slow and melancholy too. Need driving music? The Neighborhood. It'll all pass by in a happy breeze and feel like a movie scene, I promise. Need painting music? The Neighborhood. Study music? The Neighborhood. They're like a bit of everything."

Bryant shook his head. "Okay. Remind me to add them to my painting mix, and I'll give it a whirl. Movie scene like driving music, huh? We'll have to put that to the test when this rain lets up, and we take the Nymph out."

"We're going out? Like on the water?" I sat up straighter to turn and look at him.

He pulled his fingertips across the base of my neck and twirled my hair. "Well, yeah. We aren't going to see any whales at the docks. Are you good with the water? Have a little adventure, be daring."

Be daring. Isn't that what I said I felt inside but could never seem to bring out? Someone daring, someone who wanted to explore? "As long as you catch me if I trip on air and fall off the boat and drown."

Bryant leaned in closer. "I've got you. I won't ever let you fall." He pulled my back back into his chest and caught my hands in his; he wrapped them around my stomach. "You can swim though, can't you?"

"Of course I can swim! I'm just really, really bad at it." We both laughed. "So then what are we doing until the rain stops? If the rain stops."

"Oh, it'll stop," he said, "and until then we're doing this."

"And what is this?" I inquired.

"This is whatever the rain inspires us to do. Tea's gone, our hair is almost dry, you're looking exceptionally comfortable, and I'm enjoying our conversation. Especially the parts about you."

"Tell me something true." I threw back at him because I'm tired of talking about me.

He stopped breathing for a moment and tucked his nose into my temple; he inhaled slowly before sitting up straighter. "I sometimes think fate is more of a reality than faith even though I was taught faith was fate my whole life. Like when you connect with someone and you can just *feel* how right it is. A sort of invisible string that's buried deep in their body connecting your souls together and your life lines suddenly come together to share a path you can choose to walk on together if you accept that fate and stray off your own path."

I turned to look at him as his voice dropped an octave and changed the charge in the air around us.

"Are we dancing again?" I asked.

"That depends, Clary. Do you feel this thing between us the way I do?" He leaned forward as he pointed a finger from my heart to his own, his eyes hooded. "Because if you don't feel this thing between us, I think it's best to let the flame die."

Everything froze. I stared into those blue pools of icy flame because I could feel that pull. A pull that came from somewhere deep inside always begging me to come closer. Was that fate? Could I truly believe what Bryant believed, that there was a path laid before me I could just step off of to take one that twined through the middle of his instead? To let him get off the path he doesn't want to walk down and create a new one on mine? My life was planned, I had obsessed over each of my next moves. But as well as I had planned, I was lost amongst what I felt I could become in the end. Could we find our way, together?

I slammed my mouth into his on the rush of an exhale pulling a grunt out of him followed by a moan as I crawled up his lap like he encouraged me to at Central Market. His hand snaked up and twisted in my hair at the back of my neck. His other hand gripped my thigh. He pulled back gently as his lips moved down my jaw to my throat. He bit the crook of my neck and swirled his tongue over the sting then ran it back up the column of my throat before he pulled my earlobe into his mouth.

"Clary, if you want out of this dance, you have to tell me right now." His voice was tight. His hands landed on my waist, his fingertips dug into my soft flesh.

I opened my eyes to search his. What I found in their depths was a frantic necessity for an answer and so much desire. Hadn't I wondered what it must be like to be desired like this? To have someone so entranced with me that their control was wound tight and ready to snap? To feel like something more? "I've never done this dance before." I shake out between uneven breaths.

"I know. It's an easy one, but you don't have to learn any more steps than you want to." Bryant absently rubbed his thumbs over my ribs. Rhythmic. Soothing. The movements slowly released as much tension from him as he released from me. And he waited. His breathing slowed. The frenzy died.

Slowly, I pulled off the t-shirt he gave me, hands unsteady. His gaze blazed into mine and didn't move. Slowly, I reached down to the hem of the shirt he wore. I pulled the bottom up to his chest and paused; the backs of my hands grazed the dusting of thin hair on his abs. Bryant nodded and leaned forward. I pulled the shirt over his head and discarded it with mine. I drew my fingertips over his shoulders and down his chest then leaned into my hands planted on his hips and brushed my lips over his. His eyes followed my every movement but never wavered from my face.

"Show me the steps." I whispered into his mouth, emboldened by his stillness, but how patiently he waited before he was given permission to move. Granted that permission, he moved all at once.

Bryant thrust up with a growl which elicited a gasp from me just as before. He buried his face into my chest and rolled his head. He nuzzled into my breasts on a long inhale. "Fuck, Clary."

He swiftly dropped me on my back with a little bounce. A giggle escaped me a moment before his lips locked on mine again; both his hands lifted my legs over his hips before he slid his palms up my back to my bra.

"Yes?" he asked.

I couldn't speak. I nodded a vigorous agreement as he pulled the clasp free and slid the bra over my arms.

"When you stood and slipped those straps down, it was almost my undoing. You wanted to do whatever I asked. You were listening to her, to the hidden girl inside you who likes the naughty little twist, who is just as wild as she thinks everyone else is. I needed you then, I need you now." He cupped my small breasts in each hand and enclosed each nipple with his thumb; he gave a small twist. Twin electric bolts surged straight through my stomach and into my core. I lifted my hips higher around his waist. The grind pulled a moan out of my lips and into his mouth. He swallowed it and twisted again.

"These are perfect." He emphasized his proclamation when he drew one pebble into his mouth. He suckled it and swirled his tongue at the same time. My nails dug into his shoulder, and he let go of my nipple with a pop. He hissed air in through his teeth and let it out on a moan, shifting further down my body to pepper kisses over my ribs.

He grabbed both my hands in his and placed them over my head. "How about we just keep these up here, so I can show you properly just what has been playing over and over in my head since our first dance? Without losing all my control. Grab that arm of the couch and hold on, okay?"

My nod and wide grin answered him. He let go of my hands and continued to roam his way down my body. Licking first one hip then trailing across to the other and sucking in a deep draw of skin. I jumped first on a giggle then on a groan as his hands caressed my ass. His tongue continued to swirl around my hip bone as he sucked. My core pulsed and my breathing picked up. He slowly slid my sweats down my legs and trailed his hands with them. He peppered kisses down my thigh and my knee to my ankle and discarded the offending fabric working back up the other calf with his lips, then the knee, then my thigh. He paused. His eyes focused on mine as I watched his nose drift higher, and he planted a kiss right over my panties.

Bryant's eyes never left mine as he trailed his hands along the outside of my thighs and slid his hands up under the sides of my panties. He rubbed his thumbs over my hip bones, egged on by my breathy sigh.

"Please." Was all I mustered, and his focus

snapped back down. He sucked in a deep breath over my mound and those same electric bolts I felt before sparked through me. Bryant pressed down on my hips that tried desperately to climb higher off the couch with the sensation. His tongue pressed flat against my clit, right through the thin fabric before he nipped at my labia and pressed in again.

My hands gripped the arm behind me hard, and my eyes drifted closed. My hips pulled up again and begged for more pressure. He pressed me firmly back into the cushions.

"Eyes on me, princess." His husky tone made my eyes snap open. "I want you to see how much I love this." He kept his gaze on mine as he pulled down my panties and darted his tongue out to swipe my clit. My head fell back with my moan and my eyes closed again. Bryant pinched my hip with the hand still holding me steady. "Look what you do to me." His hand darted down to his pants and pushed them over his hips, freeing his penis from its captivity. He stroked it once, twice. "Eyes on me."

Satisfied his demands were met with my attention as I jumped between his eyes and his stiff dick in his hand, he smirked and lowered himself back to my apex. His dick disappeared from my view, but I could still feel his hand stroking himself against my leg as his tongue darted back out and swiped fast and stiff against my clit. I jumped. My breathing quickened, and he did it again. I squirmed in his hold and Bryant slammed his tongue against my clit and pressed a finger into me all at once. I cried out as my hands tangled in his hair. He chuckled and he curled his finger up, his tongue lazily circling my clit. The vibrations made me moan his name.

"Slow and languid right?" Bryant blew a slow breath across my clit before twirling his tongue around it. "But what about here? Do you still like it slow and languid, gazelle, or do you like it quick?"

He pulled his finger out. When he pressed back in, he had added another only to pull them out and quickly thrust in again. The thicker invasion made me wriggle again, and he picked up the pace pumping in and out as he circled my clit with his tongue, so slow compared to his fingers. The warring speeds wound me up, and I couldn't sit still anymore. I pressed Bryant's face into my sex as I thrust up into it. He chuckled, followed by a low moan and his tongue flattening out on me. He wiggled it back and forth in a tempo matching his hand. I felt my orgasm climb, but it was too high too fast. I never worked it up this fast.

"Bryant, I can't, I need—"

A growl ripped through his throat as I pleaded, and he wrapped his lips around my clit with a firm pull. I plummeted over the edge of my orgasm. He growled again against my clit and scissored his fingers. The action wrung a cry from me as my hips bucked uncontrollably.

Bryant pulled off my clit and climbed back up me to slam his mouth against mine, one hand still pumping the aftershocks of the orgasm from my jelly of a body as the other worked him once more. "Turn over." He requested.

My mind blanked. My eyes flew open, and I suddenly felt not so liquid.

"I promise. I won't hurt you, I won't press you.

Please, if you're okay, just turn over." His breathing was so rushed he could barely get it out. He held himself over me with barely controlled restraint, and I could see the pleading in his eyes, he needed something I couldn't understand. In that moment, I knew I would trust Bryant with my very existence as my mind screamed at me to listen to him.

I rolled quickly to my stomach and planted a foot on the floor, fully aware that Bryant was squeezing himself rather than stroking. He pulled my hip up with the other hand and inserted his fingers back in me. Upside down, he pressed his thumb into my clit and sank his two fingers all the way in to his last knuckle. Something in me stirred again with that angle, and I ground back against his hand making him curse.

His fingers rubbed in circles inside and out, and he stirred me up to the edge of another orgasm. He groaned and started stroking himself once more. His hips hit against me as his dick pressed through my cheeks. I felt his head pop up through the top. The frenzy he worked up in me had me grinding back against him while his other hand spread across my tailbone where he applied pressure to his head while he rocked gently through the channel he created.

"You have to come for me again, Clary, I can't hold this much longer, and I won't go until you do." He pinched his thumb down hard against my clit and pumped into me again with his fingers. The rough sensations against my clit and my ass combined with the fullness of his fingers sent me tumbling again. His balls tightened behind me, and I heard him shout before thrusting forward and stilling his own movements. His breathing was ragged as he slowed his hand inside me and slowly pulled his hips back. Bryant patted my butt and let out a long exhale.

I slumped against the cushions on my own moan, and Bryant chuckled. Cloth materialized against my back, and he slowly wiped me with one hand as he used the other to brush up my thigh and over my waist then down. Slow, barely there caresses sent goosebumps erupting in their wake. Bryant discarded the material and leaned over me; he gathered me up against his chest and pressed kisses into my spine, over my shoulders, and onto my neck. I shivered, and he kissed my neck again before nuzzling into it and dragging his hand down the center of my chest.

He vanished. I sat up, missing his warmth, to find him pulling his boxers on and opening his arms as he sat in the corner of the couch. I climbed in and put my head against his chest, fingers playing in the hair low on his hips that I barely glanced at before he took over.

"Tell me something real," he said after a few minutes, breaking the silence between us.

"I'm processing. That was really amazing."

"Those are two true things," he countered.

"Then you owe me one. Because I'm pretty sure you gave the last real answer, and now I've given you two."

He kissed the top of my head, and I looked up at him. "Two is the lucky number of the night, and I have never been more satisfied." He cracked up at his own ridiculous answer. I sat up with a huge grin and planted a kiss on his neck.

"You're okay?" he asked.

"Perfect," I replied.

"You were right."

"About what?" I asked, confusion setting into my face.

"My hand was the only thing that could top the last orgasm I had the pleasure of listening to. For now."

I swatted at his shoulder, but he caught my wrist. I slid my hand down into his palm and laced my fingers through his.

"The rain stopped," he said. "Let's go up on deck and push out."

He scooped up the shirt and sweats I had been wearing. He pulled the shirt over my head then knelt in front of me to put the pants over my legs. I put my arms through the sleeves then tied the side of the too long shirt into a knot. Bryant swiped the pants up my body and pressed a kiss to my hip then stood and folded me into his arms.

"Addicted," he breathed into my hair before pulling away. "Grab a blanket and let's go!" He spun on his heel, pulled the rest of his clothes up off the floor, and jogged up the stairs leaving me standing there to finish pulling myself together.

I couldn't help it, my face broke into a smile so big I thought it would crack. I did a giddy little stomping dance as I squealed in delight before grabbing a big, fluffy blanket off the back of a chair and sprinting after him into the night air.

Chapter Eleven

I thought that the view from the pond was amazing. So many stars freckled the sky in a way I never really had the opportunity to experience before. Annabelle had the pleasure of upper middle class parents who took her on vacations to country homes now and then, escaping the light pollution of the city. But my mom was a teacher, my dad was a mechanic, and my older sister was in grad school. We didn't have that sort of spending money available. Our vacations were short weekends in the less expensive part of uptown at Airbnbs, going to the movies or a play, or visiting the pool. The night sky still full of the haze from the street lights and so few stars. But that night on the boat? It was incredible in a way the pond view couldn't compare.

The stars on the water, a slow moving half hour out into the ocean, looked like they layered on top of each other. Some were brighter glowing crystalline orbs over clusters and layers of more stars glittering above them like someone collected a handful of stardust and simply flung it into space before doing it over and over again. Low in the sky, the Milky Way made its appearance; like a deep blue mountain cracking vertically through the sky. A pastel sunset glowed through its core stemming from the horizon in spectacular hues and covered in more speckles of twinkling light.

"The awe on your face right now makes me happy it rained." Bryant burst through my thoughts as he left the helm and leaned against a railing across from me. He had his arms crossed and head tilted as he studied me.

"I had no idea the sky could look like this, I thought the pond was incredible. But this? I'll never forget this."

Bryant pulled the blanket from my arms, and wrapped it around me. He gently pushed me backward until my knees hit a seat, and I plopped down. He pulled my chin up and brushed a feather soft kiss across my lips. "So fucking glad it rained," he said and sat on the seat next to me.

I twisted and reclined in his arms, my gaze on the stars above us. "How long can we stay out here?"

"All night, baby. But if this wind picks up anymore we'll have to go inside. It gets cold out here at night when the wind blows."

Bryant chattered on about the stars over our heads while I asked him questions about clusters I could see. He smirked at me and pointed his phone in the direction I indicated, reading aloud each result it gave and getting excited when we found something he hadn't read about before. There was an easiness about being in his arms and listening to him talk. It had been a month since Annabelle's party, and we somehow fell into an easy rhythm together.

Some time later, my eyes drifted closed, and Bryant murmured something low in my ear. He scooped me up amid protests that I could barely mutter then I felt the warm cabin air hit me. He tucked me into bed, and a few seconds later, I felt the mattress dip below me; Bryant's arm wrapped around me from behind. He pulled me into his chest, and his deep breathing in my ear lulled me back to sleep on the waves gently rocking the boat.

***

I woke up during what looked like very early sunrise hours to something tickling the tip of my nose. Cracking one eye I looked up at Bryant who peered at me with a barely contained laugh.

"Good morning sleepy gazelle." He pushed a steaming mug that smelled faintly of cinnamon forward. "I couldn't find any sugar, sorry. But I did manage to whip something up. You want a taste?" he sing-songed while wiggling the cup a little.

"Up before the sun two days in a row? You'd better talk while I drink this."

Bryant lost the restraint on his laughter and let out a hearty belt. "You're absolutely adorable in the morning when you're ornery. Finish your coffee and chuck on your swimsuit and some pants, the whales are awake too, and I made some breakfast. It's nothing like Central Market since we're on a yacht, and I didn't get to shop before coming so most of what was here we ate last night, but it's warm!" He patted my leg and planted a kiss on my forehead then dropped my bag on the bed and walked out the door leaving me to stare after him and remind myself that opposites really do attract.

Draining the rest of the delicious coffee I rummaged through my freshly dried and repacked bag for the red suit I had yet to put on. I pulled off the clothes I fell asleep in and shimmied into the one piece pausing when I spotted a soft pink mark on my hip. The one Bryant had in his mouth. His love bite left me an odd bit of satisfaction as I pulled the suit the rest of the way up and realized that the suit was high cut, and it was very visible. 'Cute cut outs' my butt, Annabelle, this thing was leaving nothing to the imagination, not that it mattered anymore.

I grabbed a pair of soft black linen pants with a belted ruffle waist and pulled them on, the ruffle peeking just up over my hips, ran a little serum through my wild hair with my fingers and wandered out of the room.

Bryant stood at a table across the kitchen leaning on a chair with his ankles crossed over one another. His white shirt was unbuttoned, and he had on a pair of black golf shorts; the combination was delicious. When he spotted me, he pitched forward a bit and just barely caught himself on the table. "Wow. You look ravishing, and that was almost really embarrassing." He pulled out the chair he leaned on, so I could sit. He helped me scoot my chair in then ran his fingers up the long open V of skin the swimsuit created and into my hair. His hand traveled across my collar bone. My breath hitched when his hand followed the equally exposed V in the front before returning to the column of my throat and pulling me against the back of the chair. He paused and stared down at me, eyes heated then leaned in and took my mouth with his.

"Mmm" he groaned. "No, Bryant, breakfast. Then whales. Breakfast and whales. Okay."

I giggled as I scooped up my spoon and added some dried cranberries from a bowl on the table to the oatmeal in front of me. "Oatmeal, perfect. I actually really love oatmeal for breakfast. It just needs a little—"

Bryant's hand materialized in front of me to pour cream into my oatmeal, and I beamed at him.

"You're really good at that," I said before stirring it together and scooping some into my mouth. I groaned around my bite as Bryant took his seat.

"I pay attention. It's hard to not pay attention to you. I want to know every single thing about you."

"You're too good to be true, you know that?" I meant it to be light, but he put his spoon down and looked at me, worry etched on his face.

"Is it too much? I'm sorry. I don't mean to be too intense. I know I'm too intense sometimes."

"Bryant, no. I didn't mean… Are you okay?" I put my spoon down. His response was so overwhelming I couldn't help but wonder where it came from.

He shook his head; the insecurity vanished behind a wall I watched go up in front of my eyes.

"Yeah. Wow, sorry. I'm glad you like it." He smiled softly and wiped his hand across the back of his neck before picking up his spoon again.

We ate our oatmeal quickly, and as soon as Bryant finished, he pulled my chair out and whisked me up on deck just in time to see the sun pulling off the horizon and into the sky. The clouds reflected a stunning hue of coral, and the water turned from crimson in the distance to blue just in front of us. I froze in place as Bryant dropped a kiss to my shoulder and leaned to wrap his arms around me.

"Stunning, isn't it? I'm sorry we missed the sunrise yesterday, and that I got you up early again today. I didn't want you to miss another one though."

"How have I lived my whole life and never actually witnessed beautiful things like this? I've seen more stunning scenes in the sky with you in three weeks than I have in the last three years combined."

"I agree," he whispered next to my ear. "Because nothing is as stunning as that sunrise on your skin."

"Cheeseball!" I laughed and spun in his arms while his eyes crinkled in the corners and his smile crept up. Then I saw one. Just one fin poking up from the water behind him. "Oh my gosh!"

Bryant turned to follow my line of vision as I swatted at his arm in my excitement.

"Yes! I hoped we were far enough out. They're coming in for breakfast. At or just after sunrise is the best. Sunset is good too, but not like sunrise."

"That's why we were having breakfast yesterday before five right by the docks. To get out here close to sunrise." Central Market and the stars were never in the picture.

"It really was. But the rain was nice," Bryant mused then pointed off toward where the other fin emerged before. "Look, mist, it's close to the surface again."

The mist increased and turned into a fountain burst as the whale's head broke the surface. It spun slightly like it was waving hello before splashing into the water. It was incredible. I turned slightly and encased Bryant in a sideways hug. "Thank you," I mumbled into his chest.

***

Several hours later we lounged on the deck as the sun rose high overhead into the sky and warmed everything. I rolled my pants up to my knees, but it still wasn't quite warm enough to lose them all together. Bryant went into the cabin to grab a couple bottles of water, and I sent a text to both my mom and to Annabelle to tell them about the whales.

My mom sent an excited text back as I expected. Anna wanted to know about Bryant's whale. Typical Anna. I told her to mind her own whale and earned a pouty emoji and a demand for coffee whenever I made it back to land, with a wink.

I was staring at that wink and grinning when Bryant emerged with a bottle of water and two glasses of ice. He set the glasses down and hovered over me. "Do I want to know?"

"Anna would like to know what size whale you have."

"What size, what? Oh! Uh, doesn't she have a girlfriend?" He looked absolutely mortified as he shoved his hands in both his pockets.

"She does. However, she's known to frequent the whale pod occasionally too." I couldn't help it, I burst out laughing somewhere between the look on his face and my terrible whale joke. I rocked forward in my seat, trying and failing to stifle my laughter with my hand.

Bryant's eyebrows rose impossibly high, and he scooped me up out of my seat. I thought he'd sit, but he strode for the staircase leading to the swim deck instead.

"Oh no, no, no, no!" I yelled from the shoulder he slung me over as we started descending.

"I think you need a cool down, Miss Monroe. What better place than the ocean?"

"But there's whales in there!" I screamed pathetically.

"They've all gone. And it's not like they'd eat you. Your pants," he said as he pulled them over my protruding bottom, "don't smell appetizing to a whale. They prefer fish."

In just my suit now I felt Bryant kick his own shorts off only seconds before I felt us falling, right into the cold ocean.

My screech was cut short, and I plunged under the surface. I took an extra second to reorient myself then kicked up, only to find Bryant lazily lounging on the swim deck, a purely satisfied look on his face.

"I've wanted to do that all morning. That swimsuit is sinful." His gaze went hot and his face split into a mischievous grin.

"That was very mean. I had no intention of actually swimming." I told him as I made my way to the swim deck to pull myself out of the icy water.

"Oh, but then I would've had to keep looking at those pants all day. Which are nice, but not nearly as nice as these." His hands caught hold of my ankles and pulled me forward, forcing my hands to drop behind me for support as he pulled my calves to his shoulders and ran his hands up the inside of my thighs.

I couldn't speak through the sensation. Instead, I pulled one foot down and splashed him with ocean water. He sputtered and jumped back, falling right off the deck and into the ocean. My smile returned as I watched him pop up to the surface and run a hand over his face. "Who needs to cool down now, Crossman?"

Laughing, I hopped off the deck before he could pull me back in and ran for the lounge. A brief glimpse over my shoulder showed me a very amused Bryant pulling out of the water shaking his head.

***

After changing into dry clothes and Bryant offering to dry my hair, which turned into a heavy make-out session, stomachs rumbled and no food was to be found. Our boat escape was forced to an end.

We puttered back into shore, slower than necessary, and stood together at the wheel. Bryant's hand held over mine as he explained what to do when we got into the marina. I felt at ease with him behind me and my hair blowing in the breeze, like I could conquer the world. Bryant made me feel alive.

We pulled the yacht in, and Bryant hopped out. He made quick work of tying it up and reached for my hand. He helped me down and scooped up my discarded bag.

We walked together all the way to my car and he tucked my bag inside then came around to my side, planted one hand on the car on each side of my shoulders, and caged me into his space.

"Are you sure I can't drive you home? Or to my home? Or all the way to California and away from all this bullshit?" He leaned his forehead on mine.

"I think you're confusing your bullshit with my eagerness to leave. Are you sure I can't drive *you* somewhere other than home?" I pushed his chin up, so I could look in his eyes.

He shook his head and cleared the unease I spotted for a fleeting moment.

"No, it's okay. Aren't I supposed to be some kind of shining knight and save you? Are you some sort of Valkyrie, here to protect me?" He pulled me in at the waist, his head high, and looked down with a lust filled grin.

"I can be your warrior, if you need me to set someone straight."

He snorted. "My demons are pretty scary, but I can handle them. I'm so glad you came down here. I can't even tell you what the last twenty-four hours has meant to me." He swooped in for a kiss, and I pushed up on my toes to pull him deeper. My stomach betrayed me by grumbling again, loudly, and Bryant pulled away with a laugh. "Go, feed your monster and call me later okay?" He planted another peck on my lips and jogged away with a wink.

Chapter Twelve

After an exhausting week of dorm shopping first with my mom, then with Annabelle, then with my sister, who came home for the weekend, Friday night felt glorious. I kicked my feet up on my headboard with a book in my hands; jazz played softly while I read Cameron and Maryanne's steamy love story. My phone interrupted me just as I reached some very questionable dirty talk. I ignored it and rolled onto my stomach, eager to see what happened next. It buzzed again. I turned it over, so I wasn't tempted to look when I heard a tap on my window.

I jumped and spun to face the window; a blast of bright blonde hair shone in the moonlight outside my window. I climbed off my bed to unlock the window. Bryant's wide, sexy grin greeted me.

"What are you doing? We have a front door, you know."

"Yeah I know." He climbed through and landed a peck on my lips. "But this is more fun. Besides, your dad is kind of scary." He pulled me in at the waist. "I missed you." He proved it with a long, slow kiss.

"I missed you, too. But if you think my dad is scary at the door, you better hope he doesn't wake up and find out you came in through the window instead," I said.

"Noted. Anyway, my dad was on a rampage when he opened my letter from a youth art tour company I applied for last month. The letter was a congratulations notice informing me I was accepted for a four month spot this fall to travel several countries and teach kids art. So, in my attempt to avoid a second dad I decided on the window which is why I'm here."

"Oh my gosh, Bryant, that's incredible! Tell me you're taking it." His eyes were twinkling at my praise, he swooped in for another kiss then his face faltered.

"I want to. I really do. But what will I do when I'm done if I can't come back here? He was very direct that if I took this instead of going straight to school in the fall, I'm done. I can't come back. He was already mad that I didn't start this spring. The tour isn't paid, it's basically an internship, and it'll go on my resume as one, so I'll at least have experience but no pay to show for it. I won't have any expenses, but I also won't make any money." My heart hurt for him. My dad would be overjoyed if I had that sort of opportunity, to see places with no costs and make a difference in kids' lives. Bryant had talent and opportunity but he had no support. I couldn't imagine what that must've been like as a child.

"I hope you're able to find a way to do it. You deserve to follow your own dreams. I understand your dad's worry. But it's your life, not his." He pulled my hands off his face and kissed the knuckles on each one.

"Thank you," he said and grinned. "Now, what were you so enthralled with over here that you ignored my call twice?" He took a step to my bed and grabbed my book quicker than I could process what he intended to do.

"No! That's nothing. Put that back."

His eyes were already skimming the open pages; a laugh burst from his wide smile.

"Well, well, well, Miss Monroe. I believe I've found your naughty side deep down in there."

I covered my eyes.

"Oh, this is bad. 'Maryanne had enough of Cameron's dominance and orders that night. She pushed him backward on the bed and grabbed his manhood in both hands.' Who calls it a 'manhood'?"

"Hey, I didn't read it before I bought it." I snatched it away from him and stuffed a bookmark in before depositing it under my bed.

"What else is under there?" he asked with a quirk of his brow.

It might've been my already wound up state, but he looked sexy standing there beside my bed in his tight black t-shirt and low slung jeans, arms crossed and face upturned. I wasn't used to that level of relaxation on

Bryant. He looked just like any other man at that moment.

"Nothing," I finally answered. "More bad dirty books and some shoes." It was true. I wasn't adventurous, remember?

"Fair enough." He shucked off his shoes before nudging them under the bed with a wink and sitting against my headboard. He opened his legs and held out his arms. I crawled into his lap and deposited my back against his chest; his arms locked around me and I relaxed into him with a deep breath.

"I figure it's the very end of June. I have two full months to keep working before I leave on the art tour. I can save that money and figure something out before I come back. Maybe I can sell some more paintings online or something. Work pay is crap, it's only part time but," he shrugged, out of steam.

"You should talk to Annabelle."

"About what?" he asked.

"Well, about what to do after. So, we're both going to the same city for school, but different schools. Annabelle's going to art school. Her grandma is an alumni at her school and pulled some strings to get her approved for off campus housing and set her up in a condo. Since I'm only going for an associates, I don't have to do housing, and we're living together. But the condo has four rooms, so we can bring in roommates to help pay the rest of the bills for the condo while we're in school, so we can focus on studying and only have to work part time. I'm willing to bet Annabelle would much prefer one of our roommates is someone we already know."

Bryant sat quiet for a few minutes. "But I won't be back until Christmas time. That leaves you without for four months. And are you sure you'd be good with that? What if you meet someone when I'm gone and in comes your gorgeous, world traveler ex. What will your boyfriend think?"

I burst out laughing and smacked my hand over my mouth as Bryant shushed me. "Who says I'm going to even survive you? I don't intend to have any other boyfriend in college, whether you're there or not."

"Who says I plan to even let you go?"

"Now who has the bad lines?" I asked, and he snaked a hand down to tickle my hip. I squirmed in his grasp, and he pulled me in tighter.

"So, I kind of thought you and Annabelle were both going to Hampton. If you aren't headed to Hampton for art, then what are you going for?"

"Literature studies. I fully intend to move to a big city somewhere and be a librarian in a gorgeous library while I work on my first novel."

"And what will that be about?" he asked.

"You know, I'm not sure anymore," I said. "I always thought I'd write about an epic love, and I had all of these ideas floating around in my brain. The rugged hero who swoops in and saves a helpless woman and makes her fall in love with his strength and caveman persona."

"Caveman persona?"

"Yeah. The whole 'You're mine and I'm going to make everyone know it, and I'm gonna put babies in you, and we'll live happily ever after' thing. It seems like that's what everyone is reading."

"That sounds awful."

"Yeah, well," I shrugged, "I'm not sure I want
to buy into that branding now." I rubbed my hands up
his arms.

"What's different?" he asked.

"Me. I feel different. And I think it's you. I
think you see me in a way that I'm unable to see
myself, and it makes me think about things differently.
It's like you can see right through everything exterior
and into me. It strips me bare, so I can see it too."

Bryant shrugged behind me. "I just see you,
Clary."

"I think you see who I'm supposed to be, not
who I am."

"And who do you want to be instead?" he asked.

"I want to be the kind of girl who takes her own
advice and goes on the art tour instead of school. But
I'm actually the girl who goes to school because she's
told to. I don't want to be her anymore." I laid my head
on his chest.

He stroked my hair in silence before saying,
"Then be her. And I'll be her too. I think I'm going to
take the tour. To hell with expectations."

"How can you be her when she's me?" I asked.

"Maybe you're my idol." He replied before closing his eyes, still stroking my hair. I fell asleep to the steady sound of his heart under my ear.

***

"Clarissa?" I heard my mothers voice ask as she shook me. I cracked my eyes open. "Why is there a boy in your bed?" Her expression was stern. Oops.

I sat up; Bryant's arms followed me and his eyes opened then spotted my mother.

"Oh, morning Mrs. M. This isn't, actually, this is exactly what it looks like. We fell asleep."

My moms fists hit her hips and she stood taller than her normal height. "I think you'd better go. But I'm not sure how you think you'll get out without my husband seeing you sneaking out the door."

Bryant stuck a thumb behind him to my window. "Maybe the way I came in?" He ducked his head into his shoulders sheepishly.

"Well, I never," my mother muttered while she turned toward my door. "Quickly. Breakfast is on the table."

My eyes bulged as I turned to Bryant.

"Good morning." He smiled. "I feel exceptionally refreshed despite your moms high blood pressure first thing."

I couldn't help the giggle that escaped me. "You'd better go before she sends my dad up here." I gave him a quick kiss on the lips and ushered him out the window.

I combed my fingers through my hair and had just found a pair of leggings when I heard a knock on the door and my dads footsteps on the tiles in front of it. I heard muffled voices and then my dad loudly exclaimed, "Of course! Good morning son, come on in. Tess! Grab another plate! Bryant is joining us!"

Smooth, Bryant. When I made it downstairs my mother stood at the bottom of the steps, eyebrows raised disapprovingly.

"I didn't do it, and he didn't ask," I stated with my hands raised. She shook her head and walked into the kitchen, but to her credit, passed my dad without a word.

"Clary!" My dad bellowed. "Bryant was just saying how he came to surprise you for breakfast, but it smelled so good in here he wondered if he could come in. Nice handshake on that boy." He pointed at Bryant who beamed and took a seat at the table.

"Did he now?" Mom muttered as she set four full glasses of juice on the table.

"Thank you, sir." Bryant said at the same time.

"None of that," Dad said. "My father was sir, I'm Mike."

"Okay, Mike, thanks for letting me come in for breakfast. This smells great, Tess." Bryant addressed my mother, now spooning food in front of him.

Her hand stopped mid air. "You're welcome to call me ma'am or Mrs. Monroe."

Dad froze with a bite of food almost to his mouth and looked between my mom and Bryant. "I think I missed something, but I'm not going to ask." He shoved the fork in his mouth and groaned with satisfaction. "That's my woman!" He blew my mom a kiss.

Bryant laughed. I caught his gaze. He beat one hand on his chest and pretended to type with his other hand. I covered my face and groaned.

"What in the heavens are you doing?" my mother asked.

"Nothing," we chimed in unison.

"Well, Bryant, we've been talking about Clary's plans all week," my dad said, "what are your plans for September?"

"Actually, I just received a letter yesterday offering me a spot for a four month art tour. It's sort of like an unpaid internship, and I'd get to travel to several different countries with a group and teach art to little kids. They fill up their school bins with supplies to keep going before we leave and do it again in the next location. It's pretty competitive, and it gives reference for liberal arts teaching on your resume. There's only seven spots each year. I was just telling Clary about it, and I've decided I'm going to accept my spot." Bryant looked excited talking about this prospect, but hesitancy remained in his voice.

"That's great!" my dad said. "I would have loved that sort of travel opportunity at your age. And to work with people doing something I loved. Now I'm stuck waiting for retirement for world travel. By then I'll be too ornery to go anywhere. What an amazing thing for a young man." My dad reached over the table and clapped Bryant on the back. Bryant had the clarity to not look completely shocked as he thanked my father again.

"I'm really proud of him for deciding to take it." I smiled at Bryant over my plate. He winked and dug back into his meal.

Chapter Thirteen

All week Bryant and I missed each other. I was with Anna somewhere or other, or he was at work trying to save as much as he could before summer ended. How sad to think we started just before it would all come to an end. Long good night phone calls and sexy lunchtime texts weren't enough with only the town separating us. What would September bring with oceans between us?

But that night, Anna lined up a birthday party for Tawny, and I just had to not run too far past pumpkin hours to see both my bestie and my guy. Bryant offered to pick me up, but that would mean date curfew by the you-still-live-in-my-house rules, so I was headed to Annabelle's on my own.

When I arrived, the party had already spilled out the side door. Anna was lucky she lived on a large corner lot with an office building on one side that closed at seven, and her neighbors lengthy backyard butted up against the edges of her yard on the other side, or surely her neighbors would have everything shut down. I weaved through people outside to get to the kitchen sliding doors; they were closest to the dance floor where I was sure to find Anna. Inside the music was loud and voracious, the energy of the people packed around counters and the make-shift dance floor matched the house beats that filled the air. I had just worked my way into the gyrating crowd when an arm snaked around me from behind. It rooted me in place and pulled the air out of me on impact.

"Now isn't this a familiar sight?" A voice like honey and low enough to almost sound menacing brushed over my ear. Bryant's lips were so close I could feel each movement against my earlobe, the light stubble from a full day between shaves rubbed over the back edge of my jaw and sent shivers down my back.

I said nothing and waited for his next move. He nuzzled his nose around the back of my ear and inhaled deeply. His teeth scraped along the ridge behind my lobe. His hands tucked themselves into the waistband of my skirt, and the tips of his fingers bit hard into my hips before his caress softened and dragged up my waist, under my shirt, and over my ribs. He skimmed the underside of my breasts before running his hands down my sides to the back side of my thighs. He slid slowly around the front of my legs and pulled me tighter against him.

"You have a funny way of asking permission," I said over my shoulder with absolutely no venom in my tone.

"I heard you like pretty boy hands on you. I dare you to tell me that's false."

I sucked in air as my core went hot. Every time we played this word game, a part of both of us emerged that was combustible together.

"And what if I said I'm not into dares? That one left me wanting for too long?"

"I would beg you to reconsider making me move my hands and let me show you what truth feels like." He punctuated his statement with a nip between my shoulder and neck and a fleeting brush of his hand up my thigh. He pulled off just as his fingertips hit home.

My knees wobbled, and I found my voice again, "What if I just came to dance?" I leaned my head on his shoulder and stared up at his deep, hooded eyes. His breath fell just as heavy as mine from his damp lips.

"Let me show you which dance I like then." Bryant gripped my hips again and pulled me tighter against his growing erection. His knees dipped as he dropped lower under me, and he ground into the back of me with a wide stance and precise hip rolls. I followed the beat and tried to stay in sync with his movements. The same intimate grind as the other dances happening around us. My hands came up over my head to hold onto him. My panties dampened with the memory of the last time he was behind me and our energies were on fire.

My shirt rode up, and Bryant took advantage of the flesh showing by running his hands up my ribs again then over my belly; he dipped into the front of my skirt ever so slightly before coming up again. A slow torture combined with his body heat and raw energy that seeped into my back.

The song changed, and the air charged with tension at the heavy, sensual beat. Bryant turned me around and spun me out; I sashayed to him as he curled his fingers to bid me forward. He grabbed a handful of my ass and slammed me into his hips and over his waiting thigh. My mouth dropped open on a silent cry, and his lips tipped up as he moved his head into my ear.

"I wonder what happens when this song is over." He nipped at my neck and kissed away the tiny sting he left. He licked his way to my collar bone where he suckled on the flesh and nipped again.

My back arched, and he used that tilt of my hips to grind his thigh higher. Bryant pressed my hips into it while we followed the beat of the song. The pressure sent waves of pleasure through me, oblivious to the room and people around us. His hands moved into the front of my shirt again; long fingers wrapped around the sides of my ribs, and his thumbs stroked up under my breast, higher and higher, until he ran the tips over my already tight nipples. I pressed down harder onto his thigh and a small gasp pulled out of me. Bryant leaned forward and caught it as another broke free when his forefinger joined his thumb for a small twist on each side, his hands hidden between our tightly joined bodies.

His kiss intensified when I rolled my hips and rubbed again. His tongue drove into my mouth with a ferocity that scraped his stubble on my chin and left a burning path in its wake. That touch of fire combined with the thrust of his hips made me cry out into his mouth; he ate the sound greedily and pinched my nipples again with a final thrust that tipped me over a shallow edge. My knees went weak. My legs trembled. Bryant held me up with one arm under my butt, and the other over my hips. He continued to roll his hips in our dance while the shallow climax subsided.

The song came to an end, and Bryant pulled my hand along with him through a throng of people. We hit the cool night time air and made it no more than two steps away from the house before I found myself backed up against it. Cat calls went out as Bryant lifted my thighs over his hips and pressed me flat into the siding; his mouth closed over mine. With a long moan, he sunk his hands into my hair, pulled my head away from his as he stared into my face.

Bryant didn't say a word as his hands went under my thighs, and he carried me to the back of the house.

"The pool house is always majorly occupied," I said when I realized where he was headed.

"Not tonight it's not. I've got the code, it's been locked since this afternoon. Anna says hi, and to have fun." He grinned wide and smacked my left cheek eliciting a little yelp from me.

He reached forward and punched the code into the electronic keypad gaining us access to the house. Kicking the door shut behind him and closing out the sounds of the party, Bryant walked us into the house and set me on the end of the kitchen counter. He pulled off each of my flats and ran his hands up the back of my calves then the inside of my thighs and back to my knees. He paused then pressed my knees open and tugged me closer to the edge of the marble.

Reaching under my skirt, he pulled my panties by the crotch; the material of the sides scraped against my hips and thighs as they fell away and elicited shivers along my spine. He grabbed my hands and held them together in front of him. Still wordless, he used my panties to wind them together and put them over his neck as he dropped to his knees.

Bryant nipped at my thighs. First one, then the other, before he ran his nose along the remaining length into my curls.

"Fucking beautiful," he mumbled and nosed my clit. I jumped, everything already sensitive from one quick orgasm. Bryant's hands came up, one to hold me to him from behind while the other gently pressed me backward onto my elbows to give him better access.

His tongue swiped from my opening up to my clit and flattened out before wiggling aggressively. I moaned and threw my head back. He stood and pulled my head up as he pressed his tongue into my mouth possessively then pulled back to demand "eyes on me."

He untied my halter and pulled the cups down to free my breasts. Bryant flicked one nipple with his middle finger and pulled the other into his mouth. He tweaked and twisted my nipple while he continued his oral assault on the other and slipped a finger from the other hand inside me. My breathy moans came faster with so many sensations mixed together. My sex contracted, and Bryant abruptly pulled me back into his hips and plucked me off the counter to stomp down the hallway.

He laid me on the bed and pulled the skirt and halter over my hips. Pressing my bound hands over my head, he demanded I grab the headboard before removing his clothes and diving back into me. His tongue speared my core while his thumb pressed fast circles into my clit. My legs shifted of their own accord at the quick motions building faster than I was used to, and Bryant pressed his shoulders into them to push my legs wider.

Sitting back on his feet, he brought my lower half with him. He draped a knee over each shoulder and held me to his face. His tongue plunged inside, and his nose slid back and forth over my clit. Byrant's movements were as frantic as my breathing. He sucked my clit between his teeth, and a slick finger swept down the seam of my cheeks. He brushed his finger up and down again, a little deeper. The sensation was too much coupled with his suckling and I burst apart.

Bryant lowered me to the bed and inserted two fingers into my heat; the action drew the orgasm out longer while he rummaged in the bedside table. Tossing a packet on the bed, he worked to release my hands then stroke himself.

I reached a hand out tentatively to touch him. He quivered and put the hand on me instead.

"Next time," he said. "I'm way too worked up for you to touch me. Fuck knows I want you to though. I want to stick it in that perfect little mouth of yours." His lips formed a cocky grin. He used his hand to move mine and encouraged me to touch myself while he touched me.

He picked up the packet again, shook it in between us, and gave me a knowing look.

I swallowed. Not because I didn't want to, but because I was so nervous. Clearly, Bryant knew how to work me, but I had no idea how to do any of it myself.

"How many girls have you done this with?" I sheepishly turned my face away; the question embarrassed me in the moment. Bryant stopped his movements and turned it back to him.

"Three," he said. "Between two relationships. The only two relationships I've had. I'm really not much of a dater."

"How do you get three with only two girlfriends?"

"The second one liked to have her girlfriend at the same time, and who am I to object? Taught me a few things." His grin went wicked, and he chuckled when my eyes widened. "I hadn't been tested since that relationship ended, but after our escapades on the yacht, I went to the doc and got a clean bill. But I'm still going to use this." He held up the packet and shook it again.

"Unless you tell me to stop. If you don't want to take this further than we already have, you don't have to."

He sat further back on his heels and waited patiently as I contemplated his offer.

"Tell me something real that's not about this moment," I said. I wanted to hear his voice again, to anchor my reality to it.

"I bought you a plane ticket today for London during fall break. That's where we'll be in September. Your dad even picked the carrier."

I reached forward and plucked the condom out of his hand and tore the packet open. Leaning forward I tentatively licked the underside of his head, just like I read in the book Bryant thought was cheesy. I swiped my tongue up and through his slit then swirled it back around to the bottom. Bryant let out a low groan, and I let the sound encourage me to wrap my hand around his base. I took a breath and pulled his head into my mouth flattening my tongue across the bottom as I sealed him in. I licked and pressed myself down; Bryant's hands moved into my hair. I bobbed twice before he pulled me off.

"Any more of that, and we won't make it to the finale. Which would be a shame, because I intend to make it a good one." His eyes were like molten sapphires, and they were fixed on my hand still holding the condom.

I came up on my knees, and he held himself in place. I pressed the ring over his head, and he pinched the top of the rubber into place for me. I held his gaze firm as I rolled the condom down his shaft. His nostrils flared at the contact with his deep inhale.

Bryant pressed me onto the pillows and nudged my legs open. Crawling between them, he laid his length across my clit and pressed forward, rubbing the ribs on the condom against me. I moaned at the foreign feel, and Bryant grabbed my chin to keep me focused on him.

When my eyes were trained back on him, he pressed his thumb into my mouth. I sucked it and flicked my tongue against the end like I had his length. He moaned and pressed deeper, pulling his thumb out to repeat the motion as he thrust against my clit again. I released another moan that had him humming. He repeated the action before he pressed down with his thumb and opened my mouth. "Are you ready?"

I nodded my head.

"Are you sure?" he asked. Another nod had his eyebrows raising at me. "You have to tell me, Clary, with words."

"I want you," I said. His lazy thrusts over my clit drove me mad.

"You want me what, gazelle?" He twirled my nipple between the damp fingers from my mouth and pulled. The wet sting cooled from the air around us when he let go, and I moaned.

"I want you in me," I replied.

"I was just in you. Twice. Lucky number." He teased and twisted again with a harder thrust.

"Fuck me, Bryant, please," I pleaded.

"With pleasure." He pulled back and thrust half way in with one fluid movement. I cried out as a guttural moan left Bryant, and he collapsed to his forearms over me. "Holy fuck." He exclaimed, holding completely still. "Shit, Clary. I dreamed of being inside you so many times. But I never could have imagined the way you'd feel on my dick would be like this. Are you okay?"

He peered down at me. His eyes lit up, his expression somehow both strained and tender at the same time. I nodded, words lost to the slightly painful feeling of him stretching and filling me; a tear escaped one eye. I blew out a deep breath, and Bryant kissed one cheek then the other. A peck landed on my nose before he pressed his forehead against mine.

"I won't move until you do," he said. He left the experience open for me to control.

"Maybe touch me?" I asked.

He carefully pressed his weight back onto his knees as he brought one hand up off the bed to palm my waist while he took a nipple into his mouth. He swirled and sucked it until I whimpered again then started massaging my hip. Still in me where he stopped half way, he pressed his thumb against my clit, rocking into it. The sensation relaxed me, and my need took hold again. The pain I felt turned into a thrumming pulse and made me draw my hips up into him in an attempt to get closer and pull him in deeper.

I gasped in a breath, and Bryant came down over me again, swooping his mouth in for a searing kiss.

"Can I move too?" he asked.

My breathy "please" pressed him the rest of the way into me before he leaned back on his feet and pulled my hips up off the bed. Holding my knees over his forearms he pulled back and pressed into me again, his gaze intent on my face. A few more strokes, and I panted; the pain replaced by mounting pleasure, the likes of which I never felt before.

Bryant picked up the pace and dropped a knee to lick his fingers and thread them around my clit. Pinching, he drug his fingers back and forth vigorously, peaking me higher. He let go abruptly and swatted my clit with a snap of his wrist, rubbing the sting back out with his thumb. When he let go and swatted it again he thrust hard to the hilt, and I toppled over the edge of my orgasm with an explosion of sensation that sent goosebumps over my shaking thighs.

I cried out, and Bryant scooped me up, turned against the headboard to put himself in a seated position and impaled me on his still hard dick. Tenting his legs he thrust up while he held me in place by my ass.

"Hold on, baby," he said, and I grabbed the headboard just in time for him to hammer into me from below. His pace was relentless, and I was liquid in his hands. When he leaned forward and bit one of my nipples, while his fingers skimmed into the line between my cheeks again, I felt the impossible stir of another orgasm.

Bryant brushed up and down my crease as he drove into me harder. When he flicked his tongue over my other nipple, wagging the hardened point back and forth, a rush of sensation swept up my spine, my core pulsed impossibly tighter, building. Tears streamed down my cheeks with the overwhelming pleasure almost pushing into pain it was wound so tight, and my legs shook uncontrollably. Bryant swatted my butt cheek. Another jolt rocketed through me with a sharp intake of breath and a moan.

"Louder. Let it out," he said and swatted again.

I cried out as intense waves of sensation rippled through me with the sting, battling for its place in line with my too sensitive vagina. I moaned as he thrust up; his balls tightened against me.

"Tell me what you want, sugar." He swatted me again, my back arched, and his mouth latched onto a nipple. A fresh sob broke past my lips joined by welling tears.

"I want—"

"You want what?"

"I want… I want you… to come for me." Each phrase punctuated by another thrust made me quake around him with oversensitivity.

"Meet me there." He swatted my ass again and slammed my hips down with his hands while he rose against me. He lifted me and bit down on my nipple as he pulled me down into his thrust again. He seated himself deep and rocked roughly against me as he held my hips clamped to him.

"Bryant!" I screamed as my climax ripped through every part of me; my skin tingled, and my pussy clenched and unclenched rapidly around him. He bounced me several times before he roared his release and pressed me down while he held his hips up. He moved in tiny jerks, desperately trying to crawl deeper as he held me to him. My body clamped around his one last time. He spasmed inside of me in return, our breathing labored and eyes locked in each other's blazing gaze.

Finally, he gathered me to him and pressed me against his chest. He peppered kisses down the side of my neck. Each brush of his lips sent aftershocks through me and rippled over his rod, still deep inside, neither of us willing to disconnect.

He whispered words between kisses, audible but my mind was too blown out to know what he said. For several long minutes, he pulled long strokes of his hands over my back as I clung to him.

Gathering my hair he pulled me off of him just far enough to look at me. "You are *so* quiet. Are you okay? How do you feel?"

He looked truly concerned. I laid there on him enjoying the feel of his hands and lips on me. "I feel incredible. I'm not sure what part of my body still has bones and is able to function."

His deep laugh lit up his face and rippled across my body, right into me where his shrinking dick pulsed with the movement.

"That feels really strange," I giggled.

Bryant snapped to attention. "Yeah, we should get that out of you. Up you go." He lifted my hips and gently deposited me on the bed. "I'm assuming you aren't on birth control?" I shook my head. "That's what I thought."

Tying off the condom, he tossed it in the trash on the way through to the bathroom. I heard the shower flip on, and a minute later Bryant returned with a dark rag, the shower still running behind him.

He pulled my legs apart as he sauntered slowly to me, and the warm cloth hit me on a sigh. He gently wiped me clean and pressed the warm cloth to my folds, massaging lightly. When he was satisfied I was clean and tended, he pulled me up.

"Let's go woman. We are far too sweaty to sleep like this, and I want to show you what it means to be mine."

"Caveman," I tossed at him.

"Oh, you bet I am," he said with a grin.

Bryant walked me into the bathroom hand in hand. Opening the shower door, he checked the water temperature then ushered me in, sealing us into a cocoon of steam behind the glass. He backed me into the spray and tipped my head back. My eyes pulled off his intense stare to close and duck under the soothing water. He pressed his body into mine and massaged my scalp while the water streamed over my hair and face.

He ran gentle kisses along my jaw and reached for the shampoo. His hands came back into my hair, and the steam hung scented in jasmine before he repeated the process with conditioner.

Grabbing a loofa I selected a soap and created citrusy suds. I ran it tentatively over Bryant's torso and followed the loofa with my hands over his pecs and abs. I felt my face heat up as I reached his thighs and drifted the loofah then my hand over his pelvis. His dick twitched when my fingers grazed it. I peeked up to find amusement in his eyes and let loose a chuckle in response.

Bryant grinned wide and stole the loofah from my hands repeating my motions. First washing over my breasts, paying special attention to my still erect nipples and sucking up my breathy moans with kisses then down my stomach and over my hips. He dipped the loofah into my thighs and scrubbed them clean. My core tightened the closer he got to it. Abandoning the loofah, he cupped my sex and gently ran his fingers through the folds. I quivered at the tingle that erupted over my skin.

"Are you okay?" he asked as my head dipped backward into the spray again and a hiss left my lips. He continued his gentle massage.

"You already asked me that," I breathed into the space between us.

"That was then. Are you still okay now?"

"Yeah, it's sore and feels swollen and strange, but I'm okay," I said through his tender cleaning.

"I didn't mean to be so rough. But you're so responsive, I lost my control when you came so hard the second time. I shouldn't have done that."

My body quivered at his touch, and I reached forward to pull him into a slow kiss, pressing my body into his open embrace; both of his arms secured around my back.

"It was perfect." I turned off the spray and opened the door. "Now, I just want to curl up beside you and go to sleep, so I can dream about the next orgasm you're going to give me."

"Yes, ma'am." Bryant grabbed a towel off the side table and wrapped me in it to gently rub me dry. When he was finished, he picked me up and wrapped me around his waist as he took my mouth in a lazy, but lust filled kiss through the room. He plopped me on the bed with a grin and pulled the blankets back. I scooted in, and he pulled me into his chest and stroked my hair until I fell asleep.

Chapter Fourteen

My nose woke me. More specifically, the smell of bacon. I knew Bryant crept out of the bed because his spot was cold, but it still smelled faintly of the soap I washed him in, and I smelled bacon.

I put on Bryant's too large t-shirt and padded out to the kitchen to find him in his tight boxer briefs at the stove. I admired his perfect butt as he bounced it to the beat of something I couldn't hear while the bacon sizzled. Sizzling bacon in front of those abs seemed like a bad idea, but I wasn't about to interrupt him to point it out. I was too wrapped up in the view.

He hummed, then jumped and drummed his hands in front of him like he was playing the pan; his head bobbed to the rhythm in a way that looked familiar.

He picked up the pan, turned, and let out a little "oh!" when he spotted me watching him. He reached up to his ear with his free hand and clicked off the earbuds. "Good morning! I didn't want to wake you up until breakfast was ready."

"This nose can't deny bacon. And it's impatient." I smirked. "And I'm glad it is. That was a fabulous demonstration in master chef skills, and I thoroughly enjoyed every second."

He smiled wide and ducked his head as he moved the bacon out of the pan onto a plate. "Everyone in the main house is still asleep. Or at least I think they are, I didn't see anyone moving but also didn't put on my pants, so I can't be sure."

I walked over to him to run a finger through his hair, and he kissed me. But I had an ulterior motive; I popped out an ear bud and caught him by surprise. His eyes shined as I popped it in my ear and clicked it on. *Stargazing* by The Neighbourhood burst into my ear drum, the refrain about their love flaming after a single spark echoed through and I couldn't stifle my surprised laugh. "You started listening to The Neighbourhood?" I asked.

"Yeah. You made a very convincing argument, and I had to see what it was all about. You're right you know, good for everything. But this song? This one is the one that reminds me of us." He pointed between us and blew me a kiss.

"So," he continued, cracking eggs into a pan and pulling out the toast that had popped up while I was listening to his ear bud, "how long do I have you today?" He waggled his eyebrows in my direction eliciting another laugh.

"I don't have any plans. Annabelle is taking Tawny to the movies whenever they get up, and I told my parents I'd be gone today. I was contemplating going with them. But if you don't have work, I'm all yours."

"Good." He scooped the eggs on my plate and came around the counter with the toast in hand. "Because I thought maybe we could go to the beach after this mighty fine meal."

I picked up my toast and added butter; Bryant's eyebrow rose.

"I pegged you for a jelly girl." He pointed his knife to the spread left ignored on the counter.

I set down my toast and knife with a clink. "You aren't planning to throw me in the ocean again, are you?"

"Hey, we jumped together." He put his hand on his chest and feigned shock at my accusation.

"If that's what you want to call it." I laughed.

"Oh, wait, I know. This is about coffee." He jumped up off his stool and poured a cup, dumping in sugar and splashing a bit of milk in it out of the fridge. Looking around, he shrugged and stuck his finger in and swirled. "Quick and easy. Here, tip that up. Good girl." He praised me. "Now, what do you say? Want to go to the beach?"

"You threw me in," I said and bolted off the stool with a squeal as he came at me. I wasn't fast enough.

Bryant hoisted me over his shoulder and planted a palm on my ass making me squeak again. He strode through the front door and around the sidewalk.

"You wouldn't!" I shrieked when I realized he was headed straight for the pool.

"Oh, I would," he said. "And this time I won't follow you in. What happened on that boat?" He craned his head around to look back at me looking over his shoulder at him.

I gave in with the threat of pool water ten minutes after I woke up. I pulled my body up off his shoulder to look him in the eyes. "You held on to me as I fell."

Bryant smiled and put me down with a kiss. "Because you threw us off." I said.

I laughed and pulled him back in for another kiss. "Eggs get cold fast, you know, and that's such a waste of bacon. Let's go eat and go to the beach." I tugged him along inside and closed the door.

***

After a cruise down the coast, watching surfers ride gorgeous waves and exploring the boardwalk, we enjoyed a light dinner and walked along the beach with a mason jar stolen from Annabelle's kitchen. We let the surf wash up on our ankles as we collected shells, slowly filling the jar to the rim. Bryant held one of my hands in his and our shoes in the other. He spoke animatedly about a new piece he was painting that was an abstract background he saw in a dream. He had no idea what would make up the subject yet, but he was so excited to see where the canvas took him.

His enthusiasm captivated me. I trained my focus on him, not missing the way his eyes actually lit up and cleared, full on in his element and without a care.

"I'm hoping it'll be finished before the studio sale at the end of August. I have a few landscape pieces ready for it, and I'm sure they'll sell. People love landscapes. But I would love another statement piece for sale on the wall. You know, since I bought the last one for charity." He smirked and looked down at me. "Will you come to the show?"

"Of course I will."

"My mom said she'd come, since it's my first big feature show outside of school, but my dad won't entertain it. He said it would encourage my defiance, and he won't be responsible for my inevitable failure. I can't tell if he's just trying to be a hardass and bully me into going to college, or if he actually means it."

"I'm so sorry. I'm sure even though he's mean about it, it probably still means something to you. It's not fair that he refuses to support your dreams. You're worth more than that." I squeezed his hand, and he smiled over at me sadly before the look left his face.

"That's okay. I'll have my favorite ladies there, that's all I need. Screw that guy."
We set into a comfortable silence as we walked back up the beach to the pier. The sun fell low on the horizon and the attractions lit up for the night. Bryant pulled out his phone and snapped a photo of me under the pier, hair blowing wild to the side, wide brimmed hat in hand, smiling at him while he beamed at me and cooed like an art director on set at a photo shoot.

Satisfied he caught what he was admiring, he set himself behind me and reached both long arms out in front of us, tucking in close for a selfie. Our faces showed pure joy. The sort of almost startling happiness seen in dreams that can't quite be forgotten; that we long to find in a world that is good at crushing your aspirations.

Bryant kissed my cheek and snapped another photo. He nuzzled into my neck making me laugh while he snapped away. He put his phone in his pocket and grabbed both sides of my face. "You're everything, did you know that?"

His stare bore right into my soul; there was nothing but truth and hope in his words.

"I love you," I said unexpectedly even to my own ears; my heart hammered in my chest. "I don't know how it happened, but I love you, Bryant Crossman."

"Thank fuck." He swooped in with a feverish kiss. He placed his forehead on mine, eyes closed, and exhaled a deep breath. "I love you, Clarissa Monroe. So much."

A squeal from further up the pier walk had me peeking over Bryant's shoulder. Anna and Tawny were just hitting the pier where it started on the sandy beach, and we were still in eyesight under it. Anna waved excitedly and kicked off her flip flops to run down the length of beach to us. She dragged a stumbling Tawny behind her who hadn't had time to take off her flip flops before Anna tugged her forward.

"I had no idea you guys would be here!" Anna wrapped me up in a hug. "The movie was over, thankfully," she screwed up her face, "and we weren't ready to head home yet since the parentals should be pulling in any minute, so we thought, hey! The lights should be just about ready to pop on at the pier and what better way to close out your nineteenth birthday than with rides and games right? And here we are headed straight for the ferris wheel when I spot that gorgeous mane of curls under this sketchy looking pier. I'd know that head anywhere. I'm so excited you're here!" She swung my hands with hers in time to her rapid fire speak, and Tawny stood cross-armed next to Bryant. Their heads leaned toward each other in quiet conversation, smirks clear to their ears.

"Happy birthday, Tawny!" I turned to her. It occurred to me that without her usual boots she was even shorter than Anna, who was shorter than me, and I was already well over half a foot shorter than Bryant. The two of them next to each other made me grin like a fool this time. "I take it the movie wasn't great given the face on that one?" I pointed our joined hands at Anna.

"Let's just say watching the goldfish I intend to win swimming around in its bag would be more interesting than that sad excuse for a romantic thriller." She rolled her eyes and grabbed Anna's free hand. "Everyone ready? I need a funnel cake like yesterday."

An hour later, we had lost Anna and Tawny in the crowd somewhere when they snuck through to get to a quarter machine so they could play in the classic arcade. I dropped the piece of Tawny's shirt I held and a stroller crept through before I could find her again, a mom and two more kids in tow behind it closed the gap. I texted Anna to have fun, and Bryant and I stared up at the ferris wheel in front of us, a bright beacon of light against the cloud filled night sky. The light reflected over the glistening ocean beneath it.

"I've never been up there," Bryant said. He pointed to the buckets at the top of the ferris wheel.

"Really? I know we're not quite uptown, but I thought everyone had been down to the pier after hours."

Bryant turned to look at me, "Nah," he said. "I mean I've been here, but not after dark usually. It's not really my friend's scene, and my parents don't think things like this are worth the time you invest in them." He swept his arms out to encompass the pure joy happening around us.

I shook my head. "Your parents really confuse me."

Bryant slung his arm across my shoulder and started forward. "What do you say, gazelle, take me up?" He smiled broadly at me.

I nodded and pulled a few remaining tickets out of my pocket. I passed them over to the attendant, and he stepped aside so we could load into each divided side of a bright blue topped bucket before it crept forward again.

Bryant leaned over the side of the bucket to look at the landscape below as we climbed over the middle of the loop up. His face lit up like a little kid on his first ride into the sky rather than the tall, maturing man sitting in front of me. I couldn't help but kick a foot out to tangle with his and draw his attention to me.

He leaned forward and his eyes sparkled like the deep blue jewels they were. I got up to join him on the other side, rocking the bucket a little; Bryant whooped with excitement. He lifted an arm so I could tuck under it, and his fingers tangled into my curls. He pulled the ends down and let them spring back up before doing it again, expending the nervous energy so visible beneath his cool exterior.

"Okay, so let me see," he broke the silence. "In the last twenty-four hours, I've had the most mind blowing sex of my early life, taken epic selfies that remind me of a movie after an afternoon well spent in soulful conversation and sunshine, my girl told me she loves me, and I'm riding in the moonlight up into the sky with a beautiful woman tucked under my arm." He stroked his chin in contemplation. "Yeah, I'd say this is probably the best day ever, and I want to repeat it everyday for at least the rest of the summer."

"Just summer?" I asked.

"At *least* through summer." He clarified with a finger in the air.

"Well that plane ticket for September would be pretty useless then." It was my turn to stroke my chin.

"Touché, Miss Monroe. Well then, at least through Christmas." He announced with a grin.

"Oh, but Christmas break is through New Years. You need a New Year's kiss. And you can't break someone's heart before Valentine's Day."

"A month with me, and you're already contemplating an entire holiday season. Have big plans for Valentine's Day?" he asked. The smile that had been building through our banter exploded over his face and deepened his dimple. I couldn't help reaching out and pressing a kiss into it.

"I love this dimple," I said.

"Thanks! I grew it all on my own." He pressed his fingers over it with a laugh.

"I've never had a boyfriend. So, no big plans for Valentine's Day. I'm just excited by the idea of being with someone for any special day really." I scooted closer to Bryant as he threaded his fingers through mine. He spun me into his lap, crossed our arms over my chest, and rested his head on my shoulder against my own.

"Let's make this day our day. June thirtieth. That's our day. The day we looked forward together can be our anniversary."

I nodded my head, and he leaned his nose into my neck, inhaling before kissing the long column. He dragged his nose up and nipped my earlobe.

"I suppose since we've been up to the top of this thing three or four times now when it comes back down again, we have to get off, and I have to take you back to your car so you can leave me, regretfully."

"I suppose you might be right. But it's only for tonight." I pushed up and kissed his cheek then settled against his chest. Our arms locked together. We watched the moon dance over the ocean from our bucket until we came back to the bottom, and it was time to leave our solitude.

Chapter Fifteen

Several evenings came and went. By Wednesday, Bryant sent me a third mussed hair, sleepy smile selfie in the morning amid protests about getting out of bed. He begged me to join him in his instead. I had to admit, I was in favor of not leaving my bed either. However, one very loud knock on the wall next door reminded me that my sister was leaving that evening, and we had a day filled with meals and malls and movies after my hastily scheduled doctor's appointment. Though hopefully not the movie Anna and Tawny saw.

As I showered I took stock of my body and realized I was no longer sore. I did have a little red mark on my inner thigh that I took smug satisfaction from, but the rest of me still felt slightly electrified and nothing more.

After dressing and tossing a little product in my hair, I bounced downstairs to find my sister at the dining table. "What has you letting your curls loose and bouncing through the house?" she asked.

"A boy!" my mom yelled from the kitchen. "And a devilishly handsome one at that." She carried in a tray of food for the table.

"What? You have a boyfriend, and you didn't tell me?" My sister's eyes lit up and shock rippled out of them.

"Am I that much of a lost cause that you're so stunned?"

"Not at all, but a boyfriend? You never mention boys, like ever."

"Well this one is something special alright," Mom chimed in. "Pretty, fancy car, he's got to be at least six-two and has blonde hair you'd never be able to match in a salon. He has manners as well. Delivers them in a sinfully smooth tone. And he bought her a painting!" My mom looked dreamily at us.

"He's really great with kids too. You should have seen him at the shelter reading to every little kid in there. They flocked to him, and he was so full of joy," I said. "And he painted that painting before he bought it." I reminded my mom. "About us." I cleared my throat as my face burned.

"I didn't know he painted that Clary. It's beautiful, but it looks sexual."

"Juicy," my sister said. She leaned in, fully invested.

"Is it?" Mom asked, awkwardly. "Sexual, I mean."

I stopped for a minute and stared at my mother; I knew what she was actually asking me. My face flamed, and I had to calm my heartbeat. I picked up my juice and took a long drink. "It's a dance, mom. A soul dance. A depiction of the energy when two people connect that are already threaded together and their souls know they've found a piece of itself inside each other. The dance that follows."

There went my heart again, and my libido. I crossed my knees and remembered Bryant on the patio asking me if we're still dancing as he pressed into me. Bryant on the dance floor asking me what happens when the song ends then bringing me to climax in a room full of people, the music throbbing through the floor and into me. "So yeah, it's an intimate painting. Our souls are bared to each other," I tell my mother, excluding the rest.

"That's beautiful," my sister said, almost as breathless as I felt.

"Quite," My mother replied. "Well I'm starved, let's dig in!"

Thankfully our discussion about my sex life was over, for a moment.

Later, I kicked my shoes off and fell into my bed. Whoever decided it was a good idea to do multiple malls and a movie *and* dinner before the airport needed to book me a massage.

I laid there in a dream cloud of comfort until I was interrupted by my phone. The loud tone came from my feet where I dropped it earlier in my haste to get off of them. I groaned and rolled to retrieve the traitorous device and punched the screen on.

I found a photo of Bryant leaning on his car. My house stood in the background. "I'm free until two tomorrow," the caption said.

Another message appeared below it.

Cross: Want a ride?

My face broke into a huge smile, and I bit my lip.

What am I riding?

I pressed send before I could talk myself out of it then buried my face in my pillow and let out a small squeal.

I heard the distinct sound of a message being typed. I peeked up and watched the three little dots bounce on my screen then stop. They started again and stopped. I heard a car door close somewhere in the distance and went to my window. A flash of light went off inside Bryant's tinted car, and my phone dinged.

I tapped open our messages and found a photo of Bryant in his backseat, nose in the air slightly, and a hand down his unbuttoned pants, his gorgeous abs on full display. Butterflies ran a channel from my nipples to the apex between my legs, like a bolt of electricity connected them and Bryant had tripped the live wire.

Cross: Whatever you want, baby.

Well then where are we going

Cross: Depends which ride you want.

What if I just want to ride the leather in your sexy car?

Cross: Then I'd say maybe we drive over to Rutherford and walk the gardens while we watch the stars come out. The sky isn't super exciting tonight, but Cheryl just put the hammock back up since it's almost live in season.

Star watching in a hammock with Bryant? That sounded blissful for an early July evening.

And what if I'm not interested in your car but still want a ride?

Cross: We might have a problem with option two because your dad is standing in the window watching me. He looks dangerous.

I burst out laughing and headed to my door. Bounding down the steps, I stopped behind my dad, toed up to his height, and planted a kiss on his cheek. "He's a good guy, Daddy." I patted him on the shoulder.

"I know he is, but it doesn't mean I have to like it, peanut." He stroked a hand down my hair. "You headed out?"

"Yeah, I think so. It sounds like Bryant wants to look at constellations. His father has a friend whose house is a bit outside of town. It's a great spot to watch the stars. We even saw some shooting stars out there a few weeks ago." I omitted there wasn't actually anyone there. Wow. Had it only been weeks ago?

"Star guy, huh? I wouldn't have figured that. Well, be safe. Have fun." My dad hugged me tight then pulled me back. He looked at me for a minute before he walked away and left me both surprised and confused. But I wasn't going to waste the loose permission he granted with no requests like curfew attached to it.

I tossed on my sneakers, having left the feet killing flats upstairs, and grabbed a sweater on my way out the door. I flew down the sidewalk as Bryant opened his door and rushed around to get mine.

"Your dad actually left. I thought he was going to come out here." Bryant chuckled as I ducked inside the door. He braced himself on the frame.

"He might have if you hadn't told me he was standing there, and I hadn't come down to tame the bear." I giggled at his mouth tipped up in a crooked smile.

"So then, where to, Miss?"

"Show me the heavens, love." I breathed and pressed up to kiss him once, twice. "A hammock sounds like a cozy retreat after the day I've had on my feet." I screwed up my face, and Bryant laughed, kissed my nose, and closed me in.

He popped in the other side and turned to me excitedly. "Your wish is my command," he declared and put the car into drive.

***

Winding down Rutherford Drive at dusk was so much different. The sun was fully gone, but the sky still held a slight blue hue. There were no lanterns lighting our path and I realized that Bryant had previously lit it just for me. A faint solar light popped up here and there where the driveway curved slightly, but it was nothing like the previous display I had enjoyed.

Bryant parked at the end of the driveway and jogged around to open my door. He leaned in the back and grabbed a lantern, flicking it on to the beautiful, peaceful lavender glow I associated with him. He handed it to me with a wink and took my other hand in his. He tucked both in his hoodie pocket while swinging a backpack on the opposite shoulder and set off down a path.

"Lead the way, Miss Monroe," he said.

I looked at him, perplexed. "I have no idea where I am. Where am I supposed to take us?"

"The only way in this garden is through." He riddled.

I shook my head but kept moving forward. We walked in silence as I looked at all the flowers, lit up like a dream in rising moonlight and soft purple. I followed paths that told me where to go until I rounded another corner and stopped, in awe of the vision before me.

This garden was different from the others. Glowing orbs were stacked in different bed levels that illuminated tall stalks of flowers and the underside of dainty shrubs. All along the path tiny pebbles glowed and lit the way forward in vivid blues, greens, and whites. Overhead, teardrops hung from the trees with single dainty lights inside. It looked magical.

"This is one of my favorite spaces out here," Bryant said. I felt his lips form the words against my ear. "It always makes me feel how you look right now. Mystified."

"That would be a good word for it," I said. My eyes didn't leave the lights, examining each in turn. "This is really incredible."

"It's for their daughter. She loves fairies. But I knew you'd love it too," Bryant said.

He tugged me forward through the lit path; he walked backward to watch me the whole way.

"These look like little moons!"

"They are little moons. And a few planets too." Bryant smiled. "Remind me to buy you some of these." He turned around and towed me away faster.

We pushed through a circular archway with vines hanging around the edges and opened up into a sparse tree line. A small cluster sat each way to the left and the right and a short distance from them both was the pond.

"Is this the same pond?" I asked.

"Yup. Same pond, just a different side." He pointed across the expanse of water. "We were over there before, closer to the house."

I followed his finger to find the house all the way around the bend of the water, the twinkling lights of the fairy garden around the bend behind us. "This place is amazing."

"One of my favorites." Bryant led me around to a hammock hanging from the outer trees on the left.

Bryant dropped his backpack and pulled out a blanket and a water bottle. Putting the bottle in his hoodie pocket, he hopped into the hammock with his left leg out and held up his arm, beckoning me forward.

I gingerly climbed in. It swayed underneath me and I let out a squeak, Bryant gently laughing in my ear as his arms wrapped around me.

"I've got you, gazelle." He pulled me in tighter and kissed the top of my head. "You know, I brought you out here because I couldn't stand another night without you," he confessed.

"I missed you, too," I said.

"I might've snuck in your window if your dad wasn't watching me like a hawk." His grin was wide while he peered down at me. "Do you think he knows I climbed up there once already?"

"I really think my dad knows literally everything sometimes," I said with wide eyes. Bryant's chuckle ruffled my hair. "No, really though, if he knew you were in there, he'd have barred the windows, so you couldn't do it again."

"Intense."

"Do you think we'll look at the same sky at night when you're gone?" I asked with a serious tone.

"Some of it will be the same," he said. "Like the dippers, or Gemini. You can look in the sky for Gemini and know I'm looking at the same one, thinking about you." He took my hand and traced the Gemini constellation twice. When he was done, he lazily pulled his hand away and slid it along my forearm and over my elbow. The tips of his fingers dragged over my bicep and he exhaled heavily in my ear.

Softly, his fingers swept across my shoulder and over my collar bone; they dipped into the top of my shirt and out again to travel to the other side. He brushed his fingertips over my nipple, his nails drug over the thin material of my shirt. My back arched into the sensation. Bryant took that as his signal to take my mouth.

The kiss was slow and tender at first, his fingers completing another loop from my bicep over my collar, into my shirt and back out, down my arm, and his nails across my nipples again. He greedily drank in each gasp and pressed his tongue into my mouth each time my nipples pebbled harder under his nails until his fingers detoured suddenly from my shirt collar to my navel.

His lips sped up, pressed harder as he grazed his knuckles under the hem of my jeans. He circled my hip bones each time he came to one and nipped my lips when I moaned.

I reached for his shirt. His abs contracted under my hands as I traced each line with a single finger. A moan sounded in his throat when I followed the sharp V that ran from one side of his body into his pants and back up again. When I sank my finger into the groove under his waistline, he growled and popped the dual buttons on my jeans. He plunged his hand inside.

Bryant cupped my sex and kneaded its lips as he purred his satisfaction into my gasped lips. "Can you handle the fire you're playing with, Clary?"

"It's already burning inside of me," I said on an exhale. Bryant sank two fingers into my folds to test my theory.

"So fucking hot." He pumped them and coaxed a moan from me. "I'd let it burn me alive as long as I got you out of it." He added a third digit, and I pressed my hips into him seeking friction.

Bryant laughed darkly and pressed his palm into my clit. The pressure was enough to take the edge off the growing ache. I ground up into his palm greedily.

His hand left my jeans suddenly, and two fingers pressed into my mouth. His other hand snaked into my shirt to roll my nipples.

"How do you taste?" He thrust into my backside when I moaned around him. I sucked his fingers, ran my tongue between them, and earned a groan from him.

"Fuck this." He cursed and removed himself from behind me, the hammock rocked with his exit. I turned to see where he went and caught sight of his dick springing free of his pants. Perfectly taught, slightly upturned and beautifully pink, it jutted out in front of me proudly.

Bryant grabbed my face on either side and pulled my gaze up to his. "Open." He pressed a thumb into my bottom lip. I licked my lips along with his thumb remembering how he liked my stumbling through this last time.

I rolled to my belly on the hammock, pulled my knees under me in a careful balance and tentatively opened my mouth. Bryant guided my mouth to his head, and I enclosed over him, my tongue caressing his length. I licked up and down the seam under his head and sank further. I tried to suck my cheeks in each time I slipped down. Bryant's groans deepened, and he swept my hair back to the nape of my neck with a little tug.

"That's gorgeous." He surged forward into my mouth with a growl and grabbed a handful of my ass under my jeans. I gagged and he pulled back before slowly pushing into my mouth on an exhale. I swirled my tongue around his head as he pulled out again. He cursed, gripped my ass, and pulled on my hair to slip out almost to the tip.

He stared down at me, cursed again, and pushed through my lips. He picked a steady pace and thrust in and out; he kept one hand in my hair to help me angle through it, the other massaged my ass and kept me firmly in place on the hammock.

He suddenly pulled out and gripped his base. He rolled his lips in and grunted in frustration, his slipping control evident on his face. "That mouth is wicked." He drawled as he laid me back and took it in a kiss.

Bryant fumbled with my jeans, undid the zipper, and pressed at the fabric. He tried and failed to get them off as the hammock swayed and rocked. Frustrated, he scooped me into his arms and set me on the ground; he disposed of my pants and panties in one swift movement.

He wrenched my shirt off next. I stood in front of him completely bare; his erection pressed against my belly, and his eyes roamed over my body. I wanted to feel mortified, but Bryant's heated gaze made me see myself in a way I've never been able to look at myself before. The fire that burned in Bryant was brighter and fiercer than the one that burned in me.

"Turn around." He said with a twirl of his finger. I sashayed my ass for show as I complied.

Bryant braced a hand on my hip, and the other at my shoulders and pushed down. I bent over the hammock and gripped the far edge to support my weight.

He dropped to his knees and pulled my legs apart. The cold air hit my exposed parts, and a shiver ran through me, amping up my anticipation. Long seconds passed, that felt like minutes, and I stood there in front of Bryant as he instructed, bent over and open as he studied me.

Then his tongue met my folds, tip pointed and pressed through onto my clit. He swayed the rigid tip back and forth. I moaned. I told him once I loved it slow on my clit, drawing my climax out. He teased me now with my admission.

I pressed backward into him as he continued his slow torture. He laughed at my impatience; the vibrations of it added a layer of pleasure. He circled my clit again and continued his leisurely pace. I panted his name into the hammock and plead for more.

"Patience," Bryant chided behind me and pressed a thumb into my wet heat. He drew my clit in hard between his teeth and moved his finger in and out, as agonizingly slow as his tongue had been. He was building pressure in me with every drag out of his thick thumb. He wound me higher with nowhere to go.

Reaching around my legs, Bryant grabbed my breasts through the braided mesh of the hammock. His fingers pressed the rough material into my nipples as he massaged with perfect precision. The bite of the material made my pussy convulse, and he picked up speed with his thumb. He bit into my inner thigh. I jumped from the unexpected nip and was rewarded with his tongue back on my clit, ravishing the little nub in untimed chaos; the day's stubble scraped across sensitive skin.

Bryant pulled away with a grunt and stood over me, both hands at my hips, and tilted me. He landed a smack on one cheek then the other. I tipped, but held tall. I groaned as a hand replaced where his mouth had been and worked me in slow circles. I felt at least two digits enter me, inch by painfully slow inch before he stopped. He kicked my feet slightly further apart then launched all at once, fast and firm, burying his fingers all the way down and plunging in and out of me.

"Fuck, Bryant!" I wailed. He pulled his fingers half way out and rubbed shallow strokes at a fevered pace over my g-spot while pinching and shaking my clit. "I'm gonna come!" I warned as the tension mounted from his pace.

Bryant leaned forward then and ran his tongue up the inside of one of my cheeks. I hissed and bucked against him as my world blew apart.

My legs shook, and my body clenched around his fingers. Bryant landed a kiss on one cheek before pulling his fingers out and slamming himself all the way home in one swift stroke. His public bone fit tightly against me. We moaned together and sat still for a satisfying moment. Bryant reached a hand around and circled my clit, still seated all the way. His stillness inside intensified the sensation of his hand on me.

"This is a sight to see little gazelle." He stroked his unoccupied hand over my hip. "And it was not my initial intention." He punctuated the declaration as he finally moved with a slow drag out and another rushed thrust in. Bryant grabbed one arm by my elbow and pulled me off the hammock into him. "But fuck me." Drag out. "Or rather, fuck you."

Another slam home made me bite off a squeak. Another slow drag out held such a contrast to the deep sensation his firm thrusts built inside me that I whined.

"Are you okay, Princess?" he asked as he plowed back through my folds.

"More." Was the only word I could croak out.

"More what, baby?"

"More. Too slow. It's not enough."

"I thought you liked it slow?" He teased and dragged out slower than before.

"Give me more, Bryant." My legs shook as I tried to press him back in, but he stilled and held me in place with both hands. My clit throbbed from the sudden lack of friction.

"What do we say?" Bryant asked. He rubbed a hand over my left cheek and I quivered in anticipation.

"Please, Bryant. Please!" I begged.

"Good girl." He cooed. He thrust to the hilt and smacked the cheek he'd just been rubbing. He dragged himself out and thrust in over and over at a much quicker pace, giving me the frenzy I desired.

I panted and mewled and felt the squeeze I was growing familiar with when Bryant barked, "Oh no, you don't!" He pulled out and turned me over. "I want to see your face when you hit the stars." Pulling the hammock closer, he grinned wide. "This ought to be fun." He wrapped my ankles around his hips, and I got one warning to hold on before he fisted the hammock and hauled me in with a sharp jolt against him.

A duet of our moans filled the air around us. Bryant rolled a shudder off his shoulders. "Too hard?" He grabbed my face and directed me to his eyes. I shook my head. "Good."

He adjusted his grip on the hammock and pulled me back in; he set a fevered pace that made him groan and growl again and again. The sounds amplified me, and I pulsed around him again.

"Come with me," He said, bringing one hand in to pinch my clit before rubbing it in circles.

My eyes shifted and I watched the stars. Bryant's face appeared in front of mine a moment before he sucked one nipple deep in his mouth. I cried out as my aching pussy clamped, and he let go with a guttural cry. His head snapped up, and his lips fused with mine as his thrusts slowed. His tongue pressed in for a slow dance with my own and we both quivered with aftershocks of our pleasure.

Wordlessly, Bryant pulled from me and righted me to sit on the edge of the hammock. He tugged his hoodie over his head and deposited it over my own. He pulled my hair free and planted a kiss on my forehead before he leveled himself and gave me a full view of his beautiful eyes.

"I love you," he said and laid another gentle kiss on my lips.

After pulling his boxers and pants up, I hadn't realized he didn't step out of them, he threw a blanket over me and crawled into the hammock. I nestled into his side and looked up at his face. Sensing my eyes, he looked at me.

"I love you, too," I exhaled.

"Of course you do!" He smiled triumphantly.

"Caveman." I giggled and snuggled in.

He kissed my head, and we drifted off to sleep under the stars once more.

Chapter Sixteen

Time passes quickly when you're trying to stop and take it all in. The moments Bryant's eyes would crinkle at the corners when he laughed or the way his whole body would animate when he was excited about something. The moments flickered right past me as I tried to memorize each of those lines in his face or how exactly his hands waved around when he described a painting or one of his dad's fits over another decision he didn't like. Or the feel of his fingers, dragging down my spine at night, as light as they could be, charging the air and making my skin prickle in their wake.

Tiny bits of perfection.

So, it was no surprise when July was suddenly over, and I stood in an airport hugging Bryant with Annabelle tugging at the backpack on my back.

"Come on!" She shouted for the third time, or was it the fourth? "If we get stuck in a super long line, and I miss overhead cabin space I'll never forgive you. I can't check this bag Clary, do you know how much these shoes are worth? Smoochie face your beau one more time and let's get up out of here. It's only four days!"

But it didn't feel like four days. Something about it felt all wrong. And four days was nearly an eternity to waste when I only had three weeks left.

"You better go before she collapses. She can't carry all that and do all that talking and walking, too. She'll stroke out." Bryant smiled and rubbed his hands up and down my arms.

"You'll still be here when I get back, right?" I looked at him skeptically.

"Yes! I said I would. Right in this spot waiting for you with a great big welcome home sign. Go. Go see your new place. Go get a job before all the local kids take them all up and you two need to do show songs during block parties with puppies performing on mini unicycles or something." That crinkle hit his eyes, and I tore my gaze away. I looked over at Anna who tapped her foot impatiently, arms crossed, with a glare going right through my head.

"See? Lover says to go so let's go!"

"Okay!" I shouted back. "You better call me before you go to bed. I mean it. I need to hear your voice."

"Cross my heart," he said, crossing my heart instead. He dropped another kiss on my lips and spun me around. "Now, have a good flight, and have fun. But not too much fun! Who's your man?"

"You are, caveman." I rolled my eyes.

"Damn straight. Good girl." He kissed me on the cheek and gave my butt a little swat. "I love you, now off you go." He propelled me forward to catch up with Anna who was practically a whole corridor in front of me already.

I looked back and waved. "I love you!" I blew him a kiss before sprinting to catch up. When we turned the corner to another terminal, and I looked back he still stood there, one hand gripping the back of his neck while he watched me go, almost looking defeated. Anna tugged me forward, and I lost sight of him.

Sitting in my aisle seat a half hour later, I turn and look at Annabelle who is deep in thought staring out the window while we wait for the trip up the runway to get in the air.

"Where's Tawny?" I ask. "Wasn't she supposed to come and put in some applications this weekend too?"

Annabelle stayed silent, so out of place to her normal bursting at the seams to get every word out self.

"Annabelle? Anna, where's Tawny?"

"I told her not to come," she said calmly. She didn't turn from the window and offered no other information.

"Okay," I drew the word out. "And why did you do that? Did something happen? Is she okay?"

"Jesus, Clarissa! I told her not to come okay? She told me she loves me, and said she was so excited to spend a whole year living with me and making a

225

home, and I freaked and told her not to come. I mean who does that? Who tells someone they have only been dating for three months they love them? I mean who even asks the girl she's been dating for *two* months to come move across the country with them for a school they aren't even going to? Why did I do that? We've been talking for a month about our new place, and then she drops the L-bomb on me and what? I'm supposed to what?" She panted, eyes wide. Half the plane turned to look at her. She hiccuped, and I pressed her shoulders down until her head met her knees. I rubbed circles on her back and shushed her.

"Breathe, Anna. It's okay. It's okay to feel. It's okay to love. It's okay to be loved. Lots of people fall in love quickly. When you know, it just becomes so obvious." I kept rubbing circles even though her breathing slowed.

"I don't want to be like them, Clary," she whispered. "I can't be like them. Their love is so toxic that it's not even love. I don't want to destroy her. I can't love her. I can't love anyone."

I was stunned. Anna's parents were in a basically loveless marriage. Anyone could see it, but they still played it off like they were madly in love with each other. I had no idea it hurt Anna so deeply.

"Is that really what you think? That you're just like them? Anna, look at me." I pulled her face up to mine and held her jaw in both hands. "You are not them. You might be made from them, but you are not them. You choose your own path, you love your own way. You are capable of amazing love. You know how I know that? Because I feel it. I love you, and I know you love me back because I feel it." I hugged her close. "Never think you aren't capable of love or that you don't deserve it back just because they can't do it right. You are Annabelle Williams, and you are capable of great things. Including love."

"What made you so wise?" she sobbed into my neck.

"I've been feeling a lot of feelings and evaluating myself."

The intercom dinged, and the captain came on to tell us to fasten our seatbelts and welcome us to our flight. Four hours to our destination. Once we got there we would connect and fly again. I reluctantly let go of Anna and linked our hands instead.

"What am I going to do?" she asked.

I switched to airplane mode and pressed my phone into her hand. "You're going to get online and book Tawny a flight because I think you love her back, and you have to face your fears."

"I love you," she said as she clicked it on, her fingers flew over the keys as she pulled up flight information.

"I love you, too, Anna, and I'm so glad I ran you over."

She looked up at me through her still damp eyes and burst out laughing before kissing me on the cheek and returning to her task.

Four hours and ten minutes later, we touched down and Anna's face lit up when Tawny texted her to thank her for the ticket in her email. She said she'd pack a bag right away and see her tomorrow, but that would be the last of my happy advice about love.

In the coming days, I fell in love with our condo, saw the love in Anna's eyes once she decided to let it in, found a job at a quiet but adorable bookstore and coffee shop combo at the end of our street, and came home to no Bryant in the airport.

Anna drove me home in silence, and I found a letter on my bed apologizing for not calling, and not coming, but not being able to find a way to tell me that his father forced him into an eight week training internship in Europe for business management or he would forfeit the second half of his spot for the art program.

He was going to miss our rendezvous in London because he was going to miss the London art stop. I wouldn't be able to see him at all while on the tour. His dad found a way to stop him from skipping college or training, likely with a sizable donation to the travel art program Bryant thought.

Bryant couldn't let him destroy his opportunity, so he left the same day we did. He didn't say goodbye, and he never called me back.

He saved his dreams by giving in to his dad, but just like that, he destroyed me in turn.

With another sob, I pulled out my phone and punched Cross. The little count next to his name showed the nineteen unanswered calls I made to him since we touched down on the West Coast four days ago. Three of them since we landed at home. He never answered, and his voicemail had been disabled.

I threw the phone at the wall when the automated voice clicked on to tell me the user had no mailbox set up once again. Before he turned it off it was the two of us in that mailbox, Bryant trying to record a greeting while I tickled him. Turning that off was another punch to my heart.

Grabbing my luggage, I pulled open my closet and took out everything I was taking with me. I removed his painting from the wall and stuffed it in the back of the empty space and slammed the door before moving on to my dresser.

When my bags were full, and I was satisfied I didn't need anything else in the immediate vicinity, I made my way to where my phone had landed. I dialed

Anna. My parents would send the rest of my things via a shipping company as we already planned. The when wouldn't matter.

"What's up boo? You miss me already?"

"When can we leave?" I asked.

"Well, Tawny has her last week of work she wants to finish, but you know me, I'm not tied down to anything but her. You do mean for the condo right? You looked pretty put out on the way home. Are you okay?"

"Perfect," I said. "I just can't be here. I'll book us all flights, the sooner the better. Pack your stuff, Anna. Let's go home."